ACTION IN LITTLE LEAF CREEK

A LITTLE LEAF CREEK COZY MYSTERY

CINDY BELL

CONTENTS

"Aren't they the cutest?" Cassie Alberta flipped to the next picture on her phone and held it out for Tessa Watters to see.

Tessa's eyes narrowed as she studied the picture of a group of children gathered together around a Christmas tree.

"What are they all so happy about?" She looked up at Cassie. "Did you bribe them to smile this much?"

"No!" Cassie laughed and flipped to the next picture. "See? They're setting up the booths at the fair for people to visit and play games in. The kids learn so much from setting it up, the community gets to gather together, and it all raises money to help the animal shelter, community center and the homeless shelter. Isn't that enough to make you smile?"

"I might be smiling, if I didn't think you were trying to sell me something." Tessa gently pushed the phone away and shook her head. "Out with it, Cassie, I know you want something."

"Listen Tessa, I know that it's hard for you to reach out and be part of the community, but since I've been in Little Leaf Creek I've seen how much value you really offer to this town. With all of your experience as a police officer, and your general knowledge about life, I really think it's selfish to hide out here instead of sharing your wisdom." Cassie sat down at the small kitchen table beside her. "Would it be so bad to come out to the Christmas Fair?"

"My wisdom?" A sharp laugh erupted from Tessa as she sat back in her chair and stared at Cassie. "You really are trying to butter me up, aren't you? Am I some kind of old sage, now?"

"Tessa." Cassie laughed. "You know what I mean."

"I know what you mean, sure. Exactly, what you mean. The problem is, you don't know what I mean, when I say no." Tessa huffed as she sank down farther in her chair. "I promised to make some cookies, not go."

"Please?" Cassie batted her eyes as she gazed at her friend. "Just this once? For me?"

"Unbelievable." Tessa laughed, then tossed a napkin across the table at her. "That's not going to work either."

"Oliver is going to be there." Cassie raised an eyebrow.

"Did you con him into it, too?" Tessa met her eyes. Her lips pursed.

"Maybe." Cassie grinned. "But I also promised him that you would be there. He's looking forward to seeing you."

"That sounds like a fib to me." Tessa stood up and walked over to a metal rack beside the stove that held several cookbooks. "Let's decide what recipe we're going to use for the gingerbread cookies."

"Is that a yes?" Cassie walked over to the counter beside her.

"If Oliver will be there, then I should be there." Tessa sighed as she chose a thick, red cookbook and flipped its well-worn cover open. "Maybe things will be less awkward between us."

"It's just going to take a little time." Cassie's fingertips tapped lightly against Tessa's shoulder. "In no time, things will be good between you two again."

"Not sure if good is the right term." Tessa

shrugged, then thumbed through the faded pages. "Alright, enough chatter, we need to get down to business. Gingerbread cookies are serious business."

"Very." Cassie's smile spread as far as it could. Her heart still raced from the uncertainty she felt when she brought up Oliver to Tessa. As she'd discovered more about their relationship, she'd become even more determined to reunite them. Tessa served as a surrogate mother to Detective Oliver Graham, no matter how much he fought it, and he served as a connection to the rest of the world for her, family, and someone to love. She needed the two of them to iron out the wrinkles that unfortunate circumstances had created between them. It would be the perfect Christmas miracle.

"We can make some without frosting, so the kids can decorate them." Tessa turned around to face Cassie. "Listen, I know what you're trying to do here. Don't think I don't know that you're only trying to help. I do want things to improve with Oliver, but I'm not sure I'm ready for stepping into the middle of a town event. Can you understand that?"

Cassie bit into her bottom lip as she attempted to hide her disappointment. She had settled into the idea that Tessa had agreed to go.

"The cookies will be delicious, and it's very kind of you to make them." Cassie smiled as she looked over the recipe. "You're already doing plenty, Tessa. I didn't mean to push too hard."

"If it wasn't for your pushing, I wouldn't be sorting things out with Oliver." Tessa offered a small smile. "Just remember, some things take time."

"I'll do my best to slow down." Cassie nodded. "I feel like I've been on a roller coaster these past few months, I wouldn't mind things settling down a bit myself."

"I imagine you wouldn't." Tessa's gaze softened. "You've been through a lot of changes."

"Yes, I have." Cassie closed her eyes for a moment as the memories of her former life washed over her. Living in high society, in a busy city, as a wife to a wealthy CEO felt like some distant memory now, but it hadn't been that long ago that she'd lost her husband.

Tessa's Collie mix, Harry, nudged his way between them to lick Cassie's hand.

"Good morning, Harry, what were you doing sleeping in?" She crouched down to pet him.

"Oh, he's been keeping a close eye on the boys outside." Tessa sighed as she turned away from the cookbook. "They've been trying to chew their way through the fence again. Silly goats. I guess they are more social than I am."

"Oh, I bet they would love to see all the kids at the fair." Cassie grinned as she looked up at her, then her enthusiasm faded. "Sorry Tessa, there I go pressuring you again."

"It's alright. I know it's just your nature to be so cheerful." Tessa gave her a light swat on the shoulder. "But you're going to have to accept that in my mind, Christmas is better spent at home with my dog and my goats. I'll have some hot chocolate and a few gingerbread cookies. That will make it the best Holiday ever."

"When I was a kid, Christmas was a pretty big deal. My mother always had the house fully decorated, and it seemed like the whole town would be in and out of the house at some time during the day. The day went so quickly, but was so much fun." Cassie shrugged. "I always thought I'd create the same thing for my kids. But Michael and I never had any. Christmas was about the only time he'd get off work, so we usually spent it on some tropical island somewhere with people that he wanted to impress."

"That doesn't sound too bad." Tessa laughed. "I don't think I'd turn down a tropical island."

"I know, I was very lucky." Cassie frowned as she

glanced away from her. "But I can't say that any sunshine-filled Christmas I spent with Michael was warmer than the Christmases I spent as a kid. It's a different kind of warmth when you're surrounded by family and friends."

"I'll have to take your word for it." Tessa met her eyes. "But this year is your chance to make Christmas your own. Maybe it doesn't need to be exactly like your mother created, and maybe it doesn't need to be on a tropical island. What do you want it to be?"

Cassie gazed back at Tessa as the question echoed through her mind. Suddenly, she felt a spark. Yes, this was her chance to create a Holiday that was just her own. New traditions for her new life.

CHAPTER 2

As Cassie stepped into the diner for her shift, thoughts of what kind of Christmas she wanted to create were still on her mind. Although she'd lived in Little Leaf Creek for less than a year, she'd already made quite a few friends that she would love to have around for the Holiday. However, she knew that Christmas could be busy for everyone. She wasn't sure who would be free, or if they would want to spend the Holiday with her.

As Cassie rounded the counter and grabbed her apron, she shifted her focus to work. Mirabel Light, the manager of the diner, had already decorated its walls and ceilings with garland, lights, and reindeer. Even Frankie, the cook, had begun wearing a reindeer-ear headband. It seemed to her that the people of Little Leaf Creek knew how to celebrate.

Cassie tied the bright green apron strings around her waist and immediately wondered if all of the baking that Tessa had been teaching her had rounded her hips more than they already were. She grinned as she realized she didn't care. There was a time when fitting into the latest fashion was important in her life, now, all she cared about were the memories that she and Tessa shared, bonding over delicious treats.

"Cassie!" Mirabel clapped her hands high above her head as she rounded the counter. "This is it! Little Leaf Creek is going to Hollywood!"

"What?" Laughter bubbled past Cassie's lips as Mirabel's enthusiasm spilled over onto her.

"Inspector Heathcliffe! They are filming an episode right here, in Little Leaf Creek!" Mirabel grabbed Cassie by the shoulders and gave her a playful shake. "Do you know what this means?"

"Okay, okay, easy." Cassie shook herself free as she laughed again. "I'm sorry, but I really don't. Is that a television show?"

"Is that a television show?" Mirabel gasped and took a step back as her eyes spread wide. "Are you really going to stand there and tell me that you've never watched Inspector Heathcliffe?"

"I'm sorry, I never have." Cassie frowned as she studied her friend and boss. "Am I missing something?"

"Only the hottest show to grace the small screen." Mirabel rolled her eyes, then leaned against the counter beside her. "I'll admit, I may be a little biased, since the writer on the show, Anton Blakes, grew up right here in Little Leaf Creek. I've been following his career ever since he left town to make it happen. We're going to have to have a binge party and watch all the seasons to get you caught up."

"Sounds like fun." Cassie grinned. "So, they're shooting an episode here?"

"On Anton Blakes' property to be exact. Well, the property belongs to his parents, but we all grew up hanging out there, so to most of us it is and will always be Anton's." Mirabel sighed. "Ah, the memories that happened there." She winked at Cassie.

"Might be more fun to hear about those." Cassie started some fresh coffee as people began to filter into the diner. "So, what does this mean?"

"It means, we're going to be busy. Everyone is going to be in here talking about it. I think I'll ask

Tamera if she can come in for a few extra shifts in case we get a little too busy." Mirabel walked over to the phone and lifted it out of its cradle.

As Mirabel made her call, Cassie walked over to greet a customer who had just settled at the counter. She recognized the baseball cap that he pulled off of his head to reveal straight, blond hair, and the smile that spread so wide across his lips that his full cheeks gave way to dimples.

"Good morning, Sebastian."

"Good morning." Sebastian Vail held her gaze as he reached for her hand. His honey sweet voice made her smile. "Sorry I missed you this morning. I know I was supposed to be by for coffee and to go over the plans for the spring garden."

"No need to apologize." Cassie stroked her thumb across the back of his hand. "I figured that you had somewhere you had to be. Besides, it seems a little strange to be planning a garden when the weatherman is predicting snow."

"It hasn't snowed here in years." Sebastian shook his head. "I doubt that's going to happen. It's never too early to plan a garden, the more time we have to think ahead, the better it'll turn out."

Cassie savored the warmth of his touch even as she pulled her hand away to pour him a cup of coffee. Sebastian's methodical mind always surprised her. His mellow nature and laid back attitude made it quite a surprise when he paid such close attention to detail and insisted on getting everything exactly the way he wanted it to be before he proceeded with any task.

"I guess you're right about that." She set the cup down in front of him. "My first winter project is to get that backsplash in the kitchen done."

"I'll be over in the morning to help you with that." Sebastian took a sip of his coffee.

"I think I might be able to do it. I've watched a few videos." Cassie looked into his eyes. "I don't want to take up all your time, especially around Christmas."

"I'm happy to do it." Sebastian raised an eyebrow. "It's pretty precise work."

Cassie winced as she recalled the number of times he'd had to help her fix her attempts at doing things herself.

"You've done so much for me, I can at least give it a try." She glanced up at the door as a customer walked in. "Excuse me."

By the time Cassie had finished seating and serving the new customer, Sebastian had left the diner.

"Sorry hon, he said to let you know to have a good day." Mirabel smiled as she joined her at the counter. "How are things going with him?"

"New, very new." Cassie shook her head. "Sometimes I think I have forgotten how to do everything when it comes to romance."

"You don't have to remember, it'll come naturally." Mirabel tilted her head toward a group of people gathered around a table. "It looks like the news has broken."

"Did they get any kind of permits?" Karen huffed as she leaned across the table. "They can't just come in here and trample through our town."

"It's on Anton's property." Avery shrugged. "They don't need permits."

Cassie recognized them both as members of the local historical society. As she walked over with a pot of coffee, the conversation grew more heated.

"I don't know how anyone can complain about this." Fred Meyers, the owner of the bar in town, sighed. "It's going to bring so much attention and revenue to our town."

"At what cost?" Karen smacked her hand against the table. "How much of our peaceful, quiet town are we willing to give up for the sake of a little bit of profit?"

"You're so short-sighted." Fred shook his head and groaned.

"The same could be said for you." Karen glared at him. "What do you think is going to happen to your business when a few new bars pop up due to the popularity that this brings to our town? I bet you will be singing a different tune then."

Cassie cleared her throat.

"Anyone need more coffee?"

"Cassie! You have to talk some sense into these people." Karen met her eyes. "Tell them what it'll be like when Little Leaf Creek turns into a hustling, bustling city."

Cassie did her best to hold back a smile. She couldn't begin to imagine Little Leaf Creek as a hustling, bustling city.

"I don't want to get into the middle of any of this. But keep in mind, it's just one episode of a television show. They never last, the show will get canceled, and everyone will move on. It's not like they'll be back again." Cassie shrugged. "Just my thoughts."

"Is that what you really think?" An unfamiliar voice from just behind her, combined with audible gasps from everyone at the table, caused a shiver to course up her spine.

CHAPTER 3

Cassie turned slowly to face the person behind her. Dread had already built up within her, as she guessed that she had somehow put her foot in her mouth. The woman who had walked up behind her was statuesque with short, blonde hair and bright blue eyes that Cassie had to admit might be the most beautiful she'd ever seen. She wore a high-end pants suit that complemented every curve and slope of her body. Sparkling jewelry hung from her ears, neck, and wrists.

"It's good to know that you've already put an expiration date on the show I produce." She held her hand out to Cassie. "I'm Sandy Reynor. I don't believe we've met."

"Cassie, I'm Cassie Alberta." Cassie tried to

swallow past the hard lump that had formed in her throat. The woman's warm hand gripped hers a little tighter than necessary. As she released it, she looked past Cassie to the group assembled at the table.

"I can see our sudden presence here has caused a little disharmony." Sandy raised an eyebrow. "Trust me, I don't want to be here either. I was led to believe that this town was going to be far different than it actually is. But we have a deadline to meet, so you are stuck with us. Complain all you want, but we aren't going anywhere." She nodded toward the pot of coffee in Cassie's hand. "Are you going to pour me some of that, or do you plan to just stand there until it cools off?"

Cassie held back a gasp as she hurried to get her a mug from behind the counter.

"Wow! That is Sandy Reynor!" Mirabel grinned as Cassie pushed past her to get to a mug. "What is she like?"

"Offended and thirsty." Cassie splashed the coffee into a mug and set it on a tray along with cream and sugar. As she hurried back over to Sandy's table, she noticed the woman sat at a table completely alone. "Ms. Reynor, I apologize if I offended you."

"Relax doll, I never leave tips anyway." Sandy rolled her eyes then focused on her phone.

Cassie frowned as she walked away from the table. Maybe the show would be good for the town, but she doubted that Sandy was the least bit concerned about whether it was or not. Perhaps Karen had reason to be worried.

As Cassie walked back over to the counter, she overheard a conversation between Mirabel and a customer at the counter. Cassie recognized him as a regular, Kelvin Green. He came into the diner most days for lunch.

"All I'm saying is that Anton took off and didn't look back." Kelvin took a sip of his coffee as he glanced at Cassie. "Maybe for someone who is not from here, that isn't a big deal, but we all know what it means to betray Little Leaf Creek like that."

"That's not really fair though, is it?" Mirabel frowned. "Anton did look back. He is the reason they're filming the show here."

"Maybe." Kelvin shrugged. "But it seems like a little too late to me. Have you been out to the house lately? I'm not sure how his parents still live there."

"I know many locals have struggled getting a job over the past few years, and that includes his father." Mirabel sighed as she glanced at Cassie. "The job market has been rough around here, especially for the older population. Businesses prefer to hire cheaper staff. Especially seeing as many of the businesses in neighboring towns have been bought out by large city companies."

"That sounds terrible." Cassie frowned. "Maybe Anton hopes this will help his parents out."

"Maybe." Kelvin cleared his throat as he eyed her. He glanced over at Sandy's table, then lowered his voice. "But Sandy, the producer of the show, I went to college with her, and she's not someone who can be trusted. The only time I left Little Leaf Creek was to get an education. Instead, I got a different kind of education. Sandy taught me that the world outside of Little Leaf Creek is filled with lowlifes, people that will do absolutely anything to get ahead. She got me kicked out of college, and I lost every penny I invested in my education. So, just think about that, when you freshen up her coffee." He tossed a few dollars down on the counter, then turned and walked out of the diner.

"He seemed so angry." Cassie looked at Mirabel.

"He is a pretty angry guy." Mirabel shook her head. "He's mostly harmless, though."

"I guess that's a relief."

Cassie felt uneasy throughout the remainder of her shift. She heard more debates between locals about the cost versus the benefit of having the show filmed there. By the time she hung up her apron, she was eager to speak with one of the most level-headed people she knew, she had a date with Sebastian.

With only a few minutes to spare when she got home, she quickly changed into a casual dress and ducked into the bathroom to check her hair. Finding it a bit frazzled from her shift, she smoothed down her brown curls and watched them spring back to life in the mirror. A few silver strands glistened in the light that shined above the bathroom mirror. Yes, forty was a breath away. Her life had been turned upside down with the death of her husband, and subsequent decision to go back to her roots by purchasing a fixer-upper farmhouse in a small town similar to the one she had grown up in. A few gray hairs were to be expected. Would Sebastian notice? She pushed the thought away. Though they had been on a few official dates, things were still quite new and there was no reason to think they would last. Other than the way her heart skipped every time she saw him. She couldn't recall ever having that feeling before.

Cassie's phone buzzed against the porcelain surface of the sink, amplifying the sound. She picked it up with a smile and read the text from Sebastian.

Won't be able to make it. Sorry for the late notice. Can't talk now.

Cassie stared at the words on the screen. It wasn't the broken date that concerned her, as much as the short sentences. What had him in such a rush? What could prevent him from even offering an explanation? Her fingertip hovered over the keyboard as she considered texting him back. She guessed she should say something like, 'no problem, hope everything is okay' but she couldn't bring herself to type it out. Her curious nature made her want to find out what exactly he was up to. She sent the thumbs up emoji before she could think it through. What kind of answer was that?

"Ugh, ridiculous, Cassie!" She looked at her reflection in the mirror. "Something came up, that's the end of it. What I need is a distraction." She grabbed her purse and headed out the door.

As Cassie drove toward the diner, her thoughts drifted once more to Sebastian. Things had sparked between them despite the fact that she had first assumed he was much younger than her. He had a youthful face, and his charming nature attracted the attention of just about every woman in Little Leaf Creek. The thought that he was interested in her, seemed impossible to her. Yet, he had insisted, and she had taken a chance. Perhaps she had been dazzled by his smooth accent and his determination.

"A milkshake will fix this." She pushed the car door shut with her hip and headed for the door of the diner.

As Mirabel had predicted, the diner had filled up with people. She could count at least twenty through the front window, and knew that the rest of the tables and booths were likely filled as well. She pulled the door open and walked into a cloud of commotion. The chatter that flew between tables centered around Inspector Heathcliffe. She hopped onto the only open seat at the counter and leaned heavily on her elbows.

"Cassie! Can't get enough of this place?" Mirabel grinned as she walked over. "I thought you had a date?"

"I thought I did, too." Cassie forced a smile. "When you're not busy, can I get a chocolate milkshake, please?"

"And can I get another of those smoothies." A man leaned against the counter beside Cassie.

One glance at him let Cassie know that he wasn't from Little Leaf Creek. Between his expensive shoes, and trendy haircut, she had no doubt that he was there with the show. It occurred to her that people probably felt the same way about her when she first arrived.

"Anything for you, Craig." Mirabel batted her eyes at him.

"Thanks." Craig glanced around at the other patrons.

Cassie studied him while he was distracted. He appeared to be in his twenties, with a boyish face and a heap of muscles. She guessed that he wouldn't be someone they would stick behind the camera.

"I'm Cassie." She smiled at him. "I guess we're both fans of Mirabel's delicious drinks."

"Huh?" Craig glanced at her. "Whatever, it's the only thing I can find around here. I can't believe how little there is in this town."

Cassie gasped as all of a sudden she recognized him.

"Craig? Craig Wethers?"

"Yes." Craig nodded. "That's me."

"I'm Cassie. Cassie Alberta. My late husband, Michael, used to work for your father."

"Really?" Craig looked more closely at her. "I think I remember him. But I don't remember you."

"I doubt you would." Cassie smiled. "You were much younger when they worked together. We only met a couple of times at the company parties."

"Dad's been retired for years. I'm surprised you remembered me." Craig shook his head.

"It took me a while." Cassie smiled. "But you look a lot like your dad."

"Thanks." Craig took the smoothie that Mirabel offered him. "Did you put the kale in it?" He sniffed the green drink.

"Sure did." Mirabel patted his hand. "Plenty of it."

"Great." Craig tossed a one hundred dollar bill down on the counter then settled in a spot at the counter that had just opened up.

"Wow." Cassie's eyes widened as Mirabel pocketed the tip. "I can definitely see the advantages of the show being filmed here. Is he an actor in the show?"

Mirabel handed Cassie her milkshake, walked around the side of the counter closer to Cassie and lowered her voice.

"He plays a small role on the show. He's not really that great of an actor. I think they just keep him on the show for eye candy. From the gossip I've overheard, he seems to be the producer's favorite at the moment. I think they're seeing each other." Mirabel rolled her eyes. "Are you sure you're okay with Sebastian breaking your date tonight? It's pretty rude."

"I'm sure he has his reasons." Cassie sighed as she savored her milkshake. "Besides, we've just started dating."

"Which means he should be making a good impression." Mirabel clucked her tongue.

CHAPTER 4

Cassie woke up the next morning to the memory of Mirabel's clucking tongue. She'd had a hard time falling asleep as she checked her phone over and over again to see if Sebastian texted. Nothing. She grabbed her phone and checked it before her eyes were even fully open. Nothing.

Cassie's heart dropped. Had she done something to lose his interest? Had she been right from the beginning to think it was crazy for someone as handsome and charming as him to be interested in someone like her? She winced as her mind and emotions swirled into a thick cloud of dread. Maybe it was best that he'd lost interest now, before things could get too serious.

Determined to put him out of her mind, Cassie

headed straight to the kitchen and the box of tiles that waited to be put up on the wall. A short time later, she'd managed to get a few in place, but the farther she got from the edge of the wall the harder it became.

"Just straighten out!" Cassie huffed as she tried to slide the already drying tile into the right place on the wall behind her kitchen sink. Her muscles flexed as she leaned her weight into the tile. It popped off the wall and clanged into the metal sink as she lost her balance from the force. "Ugh!" She squeezed her eyes shut as frustration boiled within her.

As much as she tried not to, she wished that Sebastian would just show up. He was a farmer and he seemed to be skilled at just about everything. When she'd first moved to Little Leaf Creek he'd insisted his way into helping her get her home into shape. Usually, he showed up before she even thought about picking up a hammer, or spotted a leaking pipe.

Cassie glanced toward the door and sighed.

"This time you're going to have to figure this out yourself, Cassie." She wiped her hands clean, then took a step back to assess the damage. The tile itself appeared unharmed, but the wall would require some sanding before she could attempt to place the tile again.

"Break time." Cassie shook her head as she walked away from the mess. Although she enjoyed a challenge, she also knew when she'd had enough. She tied her hair up as she descended the front steps of her house, then headed for the shared gate that separated her and Tessa's yard. The moment she crossed the property line, two furry creatures bolted straight toward her.

"Morning Gerry and Billy!" Cassie laughed as the goats nuzzled her hands in search of treats. "Sorry, I didn't bring anything this morning." She gave them each a pet. She never thought that she would live next to two goats, let alone grow so fond of them. "Wow! You two look so clean!" She took a hesitant sniff. "Oh, and you smell great, too. Did you have baths?"

The goats stared into her eyes and backed away from her.

Cassie laughed. "Did I say something wrong?" She walked past them and up the steps of Tessa's back porch.

Each morning, Cassie knew where Tessa would be. She spent a good amount of time in her kitchen, watching the tiny television on her counter and sipping coffee.

"Morning Tessa!" She poked her head through the door and smiled. Harry ran over to the door with his tail wagging. Cassie crouched down to greet him. "Morning pup."

"It's about time you showed up." Tessa set a pile of cookie sheets down on the counter with a clatter. "I thought maybe you got distracted with Sebastian."

"No such luck." Cassie pursed her lips, then forced a smile. "I did however discover that I am not good at putting tiles on walls. I thought I could handle the backsplash on my own, but I'm starting to doubt my skills."

"No, no, none of that." Tessa turned to face her. "I'm sure you can do it if you stick with it."

"You're right, I probably can. But it would be a lot more fun if I had Sebastian beside me." Cassie sat down at the kitchen table. "He canceled our date last night at the last minute, and I haven't heard from him since."

"Doesn't sound like him." Tessa narrowed her eyes.

"I agree. I'm sure it's nothing too serious, but something is definitely going on." Cassie eyed the cookie sheets. "Are we ready to get started?"

"We'd better, we have a lot to make. I already have a batch of dough in the refrigerator because it needs to cool. I tweaked the recipe a bit." Tessa glanced over at her. "So, did any of the people from the show come into the diner yesterday?"

"Oh yes. The producer, and an actor on the show named Craig. Interesting people." Cassie smiled. "Michael actually used to work for Craig's father, can you believe it. It was years ago. I used to play with the kids at the company parties." She laughed. "It was more fun than making small talk with the adults. I recognized him but he didn't recognize me."

"Small world. You didn't meet the assistant producer, Nel, though? She wasn't there?" Tessa lined the pans up on the counter while Cassie got out a large bowl and some of the ingredients for the cookies.

"No. Are you a fan of hers?"

"Absolutely. I've read all about her in interviews. She keeps things so accurate on the show. I'm quite impressed with how well they reflect the behavior of actual police." Tessa pointed to the pantry. "We need flour and brown sugar, I've already set the butter out to soften."

Cassie felt some relief as she piled the ingredients on the counter. Although, she was determined to get the backsplash done, she felt much more confident about making cookies with Tessa.

"I noticed that Gerry and Billy had a bath." Cassie glanced over at her. "Any particular reason?"

"I blame you." Tessa locked eyes with Cassie's. "Somehow you managed to convince me to be part of the Christmas Fair. I signed the goats up to be part of the petting zoo."

"Yes!" Cassie grinned as she clapped her hands. Harry ran over at the sound. "You're not going to regret this, Tessa!" Cassie gave Harry a treat.

"I already do." Tessa moaned. "Now, let's get moving, these cookies aren't going to make themselves. We'll need to make quite a few, and the dough needs to cool in the refrigerator, so we won't get them all done today."

Cassie reached into her pocket to check her phone. She just wanted to see if Sebastian had texted. But as she caught sight of Tessa's determined stare, she focused on getting the ingredients into the bowl instead.

CHAPTER 5

After getting the first batch of cookies into the oven, Cassie walked over to Harry, who was lying in his bed in the corner of the kitchen. She gave him a light pat on the head and a treat, then headed for the diner for her late morning shift. Despite spending most of her adult life as a wealthy socialite, who managed a small museum, she'd chosen to take a job as a waitress.

Her first job, in the small town she'd grown up in, was working in a diner. She thought it might round out her experience of getting back to her roots. But she'd soon discovered that it wasn't so easy to pick up right where she'd left off. Keeping up with the orders and great customer service came straight back to her. But her feet ached more and she had dropped a few trays. But she never thought about quitting. She loved working with Mirabel and working at the diner helped make her feel part of the community.

"Morning Mirabel." Cassie smiled as she walked around behind the front counter.

"Cassie! I was just thinking about you." Mirabel smiled as she tossed her long braid over her shoulder. "Not because you're late, really."

"I'm sorry." Cassie winced. "I got caught up making cookies with Tessa."

"I'm just teasing you, you're not late." Mirabel gave her shoulder a playful shove.

It was Mirabel, and her infectious cheerfulness, that made the job fun.

"Remember that actor I told you about? The one that I have a huge crush on." Mirabel grinned. "Lionel."

"You sent me about a hundred pictures." Cassie laughed at the way Mirabel was acting like a teenager.

"He's here!" Mirabel squeaked out her words as her cheeks reddened. "Right here in the diner!"

"Really?" Cassie glanced over the busy diner. "Where?"

"Over there." Mirabel nudged her with her elbow. "See? I told you he was handsome."

"He is." Cassie smiled as she studied the two men and one woman gathered around a small table near the front window. The tallest one she recognized as Lionel, she couldn't miss him, considering she'd received a photograph of him from just about every angle, from Mirabel. He played the role of the partner to the main star of the show. "Who is he with?"

"One of them is his brother, Simon. He's stuck to him like glue, according to all of the fan magazines. The other is Nel, she's the assistant producer on the show. She's very well-liked by all of the actors and actresses. At least, from what I've read and heard she is." Mirabel slid a tray of drinks toward her. "Can you please take these over to them? I just know if I do it, I'll end up spilling something on someone. I don't want Lionel to know what a huge fan I am."

"Of course." Cassie couldn't resist a smile. Seeing Mirabel flustered was new for her. The usually self-assured woman blushed as she turned away from the counter.

Cassie picked up the tray. If she could get Lionel's autograph, she knew that Mirabel would love to have it, and would never dare to ask for it.

Although, Mirabel was confident and outgoing, she was obviously flustered by his presence.

"Hello there." She smiled as she paused beside their table. "My name is Cassie, and I'll be taking over as your server."

"Oh?" Lionel looked toward the counter. "Too bad, the lady that seated us was such a sweetheart."

"She's actually the manager." Cassie set Lionel's glass down in front of him.

"I see." Lionel grinned, then glanced at the other two people seated around the table. "I guess we should be honored that she seated us."

"I am." Simon laughed as he took his glass from Cassie's hand. "I have to say, the people of this town are hard to figure out. It seems like half of you don't want us here, and the other half are excited. So, which are you, Cassie?"

Cassie set the final glass down in front of Nel and looked between the three as she spoke.

"I actually had never heard of the show before you arrived, but I'm sure that you all do a fantastic job and it's great. In fact, I've heard wonderful things about your acting, Lionel, and in particular about the authenticity that you bring to the show, Nel."

"That's a relief." Simon took a sip of his water. "This isn't from the tap, is it?"

"No." Cassie leaned in close and whispered, "It's direct from the spring that runs through the yard out back. Only the best for our Hollywood guests."

Simon spit out his sip of water.

Nel lost a few drops of hers as well as she laughed.

"Oh, she's funny. I like her."

"Sorry." Cassie winced as she handed Simon a napkin. "My sense of humor gets away from me sometimes."

"Clever." Simon eyed her as he mopped up his tie with the napkin.

"You may not be a huge fan of the show, Cassie, but I think you have a few fans of your own already." Lionel winked at her, then placed his order.

As Cassie jotted down their orders, she noticed the three of them look toward the door of the diner.

"What is he doing here?" Lionel muttered his words to Nel. "If Sandy gets her hands on him, he's not going to survive the night."

Cassie barely noticed their exchange as her focus was on the window that overlooked the street outside the diner. She watched as Sebastian and a woman she'd never seen before exchanged heated words. She'd never seen him look so upset before. To her shock, he grabbed the woman's arm and pulled her toward his pickup truck.

The woman, as blonde as Sebastian, and about the same age, didn't resist, but appeared to continue to argue with him until they got into the truck. He pulled his truck away from the curb with a roar of the engine.

Cassie's heart skipped a beat as she wondered what she'd just witnessed. Perfectly calm Sebastian, losing his mind over a beautiful woman? Was this the reason that he hadn't texted her back?

"Cassie." Lionel's voice drew her attention. "That's your name, right?"

"Yes." Cassie blinked as she looked back at him. "I'm sorry."

"Can you make sure Anton is seated with us." Lionel tipped his head toward the man still waiting by the door.

"Sure, of course." Cassie walked over to him, her mind still spinning. "Anton?"

"Yes." Anton met her eyes. "I'm sorry, I don't remember you. Did we go to high school together?"

"No." Cassie smiled. "I'm fairly new to town. But the gentleman at that table, asked me to seat you there." She pointed to Lionel's table.

"Perfect." Anton groaned, then walked reluctantly over to the table.

"Well, if it isn't the man of the hour." Lionel chuckled and clapped Anton's arm hard. "What a major mess, huh? Sandy might just kill you."

"It's not that bad. She's just being dramatic." Anton crossed his arms.

"The whole point of filming here was so she could avoid having to build a set or rent out an expensive piece of land. Now, she's going to have to do some rebuilding to get what she needs from the property. You lied to her about your parents' house, didn't you? You told me all about the place, and I saw all the pictures that you sent her of the property and the house. Just how old were those pictures? Did you mention how bad the place stunk?"

"It's fine!" Anton glared at Lionel. "If she wouldn't be so picky about everything, this episode would already be finished!"

"I do like the location." Nel spoke up as she pushed out a chair toward Anton. "I think it's gritty, and a real example of how families are facing financial hardships and what's going on with their properties as a result. I'll try to talk to her about it, so she's not so hard on you, alright?"

"Thanks Nel." Anton sank down into the chair and sighed. "She wants to see me tonight. I don't think the meeting is going to go too well."

"She'll make do." Lionel shrugged. "She has to. We're all already here, and so is the equipment. I just hope you get out of this what you want, Anton."

"Me too." Anton glanced at Cassie. "A caramel milkshake please."

"Coming right up." Cassie headed behind the counter. She focused on making Anton the most rich and delicious milkshake she could, in an attempt to brighten his day.

Once Cassie got home after her shift had ended, she sprawled out across her bed and did her best to ignore her aching feet. Did they hurt because she'd worked so hard, or just because of nearly being forty? She could recall people claiming that after forty everything started hurting. She pushed the thought away and instead checked her phone.

Still, not a single text from Sebastian, but she had received a few more pictures of Lionel from Mirabel. She closed her eyes and willed herself to go to sleep. After Anton drank his milkshake, he'd spoken to Nel and she requested that Mirabel's Diner be the on-set caterer for the filming of the episode. Mirabel was thrilled, and asked Cassie to join her early in the morning to get things set up for the crew. That meant waking at dawn, which meant she really needed to sleep. But every time she closed her eyes, she heard the roar of Sebastian's engine.

CHAPTER 6

"Cassie, are you awake?" Mirabel nudged her shoulder with her hand.

"I'm sorry." Cassie covered a yawn as she straightened up in her seat.

"It's alright. We're here, but I think we should take a look around to figure out where we're going to set up before we start unloading. The ground is pretty uneven." Mirabel opened the door on the van she used for catering and stepped out.

Cassie managed to make her way out of the van, despite the urge to fall back to sleep. She still hadn't received any texts from Sebastian, but she was determined not to dwell on that. She followed Mirabel toward the dilapidated house positioned in the center of sprawling, mostly untended land.

"It's so overgrown, I can see why Sandy was upset." Cassie caught up with Mirabel.

"It is. I guess Anton's parents weren't able to keep up with it." Mirabel clucked her tongue. "What a shame."

"Maybe the crew will do some clean up." Cassie settled her gaze on the house itself. "Are Anton's parents here now?" She pointed to a car parked in the driveway.

"No, they are staying in a hotel during production." Mirabel paused beside the sagging porch. "According to this map Sandy gave me, we can set up to the left of the house and won't interfere with the filming." She peeked around the side of the house. "Not sure that we can set up here though, there's a lot of brush growing up."

"Maybe over there?" Cassie pointed to a shed. Its ceiling had caved in halfway.

"That could work." Mirabel smiled. "Let me check it out."

Cassie nodded, then leaned against the side of the house. She closed her eyes for just a second. As the urge to sleep tugged on her mind, she forced her eyes back open. She didn't want to let Mirabel down. She took a step toward her just as Mirabel stopped at the open door of the shed.

"Cassie!" Mirabel gasped.

"What is it?" Cassie followed Mirabel's line of sight.

Mirabel stared at something colorful on the floor in the doorway of the shed, something pink and blue sparkled. When Cassie took a closer look, she recognized it as a small, glittery purse, clutched in someone's hand.

"Oh!" Cassie gasped as her sleepy mind began to make the connection.

"Cassie!" Mirabel pushed back the door enough to reveal Sandy's body sprawled across the floor.

Mirabel's screaming sent a jolt up Cassie's spine.

"Cassie! Is that Sandy?"

"Yes, it is."

With her heart in her throat Cassie grabbed Mirabel's hand, she pulled her phone out of her pocket with her other one. Her hand trembled as she called Detective Oliver Graham's number. Was it possible that she was still asleep? That this was all some kind of nightmare? Surely, she hadn't just come across another dead body?

Cassie cringed as she got Oliver's voicemail. She stumbled over her words as she tried to explain the situation in the message. She ended the call and called 911. She once again had trouble explaining what was happening. "The police are on their way." She ended the call and held the phone tightly in her hand.

"No! No! I can't!" Mirabel turned and ran toward the woods.

"Mirabel, wait!" Cassie gasped as she watched the woman disappear between the trees. She looked back at Sandy, then toward the trees, uncertain whether to go after Mirabel, or wait for the police. She didn't have long to make her choice before she heard a car pull up, followed by sirens indicating more were on their way.

Frozen by a mixture of fear and indecision, Cassie stared down at Sandy.

"Cassie, take a step back." A strong grip closed around her elbow and tugged her backwards. She looked up to see a police officer she recognized.

"Patrick." Cassie glanced at him as she stumbled back a few steps. "I'm so glad that you're here!"

"Are you okay?" Patrick searched her eyes for a long moment, then looked back toward the victim. "Do you know what happened here?"

"That's Sandy Reynor, she's the producer of Inspector Heathcliffe." Cassie scanned the nearby trees. "Mirabel took off running somewhere, we have to make sure that she's okay."

"I'll send another officer to look for her." Patrick nodded to one of the men who stood not far from him. "There's another witness, Mirabel. She's run into the woods. Take it easy, she's probably pretty shaken up."

"Will do." The officer jogged off toward the woods.

"Cassie, why did Mirabel run off? Did you see Sandy's attacker?" Patrick looked around in all directions. "Cassie!"

"No, I don't know." Cassie shook her head. "I didn't see anyone."

Cassie heard another car pull up. She looked over Patrick's shoulder to see Oliver stepping out of his car. He ran toward them. His tall, muscular frame and confidence immediately made Cassie feel safer.

Oliver looked at Cassie briefly, then turned toward Patrick to get an update from him.

"Are you okay, Cassie?" Oliver's eyes locked to hers. "Cassie?"

Cassie glanced around the trees.

"I am okay." Cassie took a sharp breath, then focused on him. "I'm sorry, I'm just worried about Mirabel."

"Don't worry, the officer will find her." Oliver nodded. "Did you see anything?"

"No." Cassie looked away from his sharp, gray eyes as her heart pounded. "No, we didn't see anything. We were bringing breakfast for the crew. We wanted to work out where to set up, so we left everything in the van and walked over here to find a spot. And—" Her voice trembled as she continued. "And this is how we found her. I have to find Mirabel. She saw her first. She was so frightened!" She turned toward the woods.

"No, you don't." Oliver caught her wrist and held it firmly as she looked back at him. "We have no idea if the killer is still around. I can't let you go wander off into the woods."

"But I have to find her!" Cassie jerked her hand away from him. "Unless you plan to arrest me?"

"Cassie." Oliver heaved a heavy sigh, then pointed to the trees. "Look, there she is. Glenn has her, alright? She's just fine."

"Mirabel!" Cassie ran toward her as her heart raced.

"Cassie, I'm so sorry!" Mirabel flung her arms around her. "I just panicked!"

"It's okay, Mirabel, I'm just glad you're okay." Cassie hugged her tight. In that moment she felt a burst of the warmth that she recalled from the little town she had once lived in. She and Mirabel had certainly become friends, but now she realized, they might just be more like family than she knew.

"Mirabel, Cassie said that you two didn't see or hear anything, is that true?"

"Yes, it's true." Mirabel frowned as she pulled out of Cassie's grasp. "When I pulled up, the area was quiet, I thought we were the first people to arrive. I saw the car but presumed it belonged to Anton's parents."

"What's going on here?" Anton's voice drew all of their attention as he walked toward them.

"Anton." Oliver stepped in front of him before he could reach Sandy's body. "When did you arrive?"

"Just now." Anton glanced back at his car parked beside the catering van, then looked back at Oliver. "I came early to meet with Sandy. Her car is here. Where is she?" He frowned as he looked from the car parked in the driveway to the officers gathered near the shed. "What is going on here? Why are the police here?"

"Anton, it's terrible." Mirabel gulped as fresh tears coursed down her cheeks. "It's Sandy."

"What?" Anton narrowed his eyes. "What are you saying? You're not making any sense."

"When was the last time you saw Sandy, Anton?" Oliver stepped closer to him.

Cassie detected a shift in his demeanor, from a comforting friend, to a stern detective.

"Last night." Anton looked toward the officers again. "What is it? Is she okay?"

"I'm afraid not." Oliver shook his head, then put one hand on Anton's shoulder. "She's been killed, Anton."

"What?" Anton's voice faded as he drew a sharp breath. "No, that's not possible! I was supposed to meet with her this morning! Everyone will be here soon. No, she can't be dead!"

"I'm so sorry, Anton." Mirabel reached for his hand.

"Don't!" Anton stepped back out of Mirabel's reach. He stared at the ground, then abruptly looked up at Oliver. "Are you sure she's dead? Are you sure it's not some kind of mistake?"

"She's dead, Anton." Cassie frowned. "I saw her myself, so did Mirabel."

"Can I speak with you for a few minutes?" Oliver caught Anton by the arm and steered him toward a quieter area.

Mirabel started back toward the van.

"We should set up the food, Cassie, for the officers. They will need it."

Cassie nodded, then looked toward the driveway as she heard an engine roar toward the house. Part of her hoped it would be Sebastian, he always seemed to show up when she needed him. Instead, it was another police car.

fter Cassie helped Mirabel set up the food, Mirabel went home, she looked like she was still in shock. Cassie hoped to get some more information about the murder by staying at the scene. She soon realized that she wouldn't find out much, so she caught a ride home with one of the police officers. She knew it would take quite some time before any conclusions were drawn in the investigation, and Oliver needed to focus on the case without her peppering him with questions. However, she was eager to discuss it with the person she'd come to trust most when it came to figuring things out.

"Cassie!" Tessa opened her front door as Cassie climbed the steps to the front porch. Harry bounded from the back of the house, up the porch and into the house with Cassie. "I was just about to leave to go find you. I heard what happened on the police scanner. Are you okay?"

"Yes, I'm okay." Cassie slumped down in one of the chairs at the kitchen table, then rubbed behind Harry's ears. "I just can't believe what happened."

"Me either. I can't believe you found another dead body." Tessa sat down beside her. "Was it really Sandy?"

"Yes, I'm afraid it was." Cassie took a breath, then launched into the story. "Mirabel wanted to get to the property early so we could have breakfast set up for the crew. While we were looking for a place to set up, she found Sandy in the doorway of the shed." Harry nuzzled her hand as if sensing she needed comforting. "And Mirabel, she was so terrified." Cassie frowned as she leaned closer to Tessa. "But I'm not sure what she was scared of, exactly. She took off running the moment I called the police. It was like she was in a pure panic."

"Never mind that." Tessa shook her head. "We can figure that out later. Right now we need to figure out who killed Sandy."

"Oh, I don't know, Tessa." Cassie sighed as she sat back in her chair. "How could we possibly know?

She's not even from around here. We have no idea who could have done it."

"I think we may have some idea. It's important that we find out, because otherwise all of our friends and neighbors will be put under the microscope. Everyone that came here with the show will have access to good lawyers, and plenty of money to protect themselves." Tessa shook her head. "This is our opportunity to do what we can to level the playing field."

"It's not a game." Cassie narrowed her eyes. "A woman is dead, Tessa."

"I know that. But the best thing to do to help her and get justice, is to try and help solve the crime." Tessa rapped her knuckles against the table. "What we need to do now is relax our minds and try to sort through this."

"How?" Cassie watched as she stood up from the table.

"Baking." Tessa walked over to the counter. "Baking always helps me sort through things. Sometimes cooking helps as well. But most of the time baking does the trick. Getting lost in the task helps organize my thoughts. It's like you, and your lists." She smiled as Cassie pulled a notebook from her purse and set it on the table. "It helps focus the mind."

"You're right." Cassie drew a deep breath. "When I start to panic, a list helps me refocus on the task at hand." She began to write down what she had seen and experienced at Anton's house. "Who do you think should be top on our list of suspects?"

"Anton, of course." Tessa sighed as she tossed some butter into a bowl. "I wish it weren't the case, but the murder took place on his parents' land."

"And we know that Sandy had a problem with Anton. In fact, people thought she might be angry enough to kill him." Cassie scrawled down his name. "Of course, that was probably not meant to be taken literally."

"Of course not, but it indicates the level of animosity between the two." Tessa began to beat the butter. "Can you grab me that egg please?" She pointed to an egg in a small bowl on the counter. "It should be warm enough."

"Sure." Cassie handed over the egg. "Anton also showed up right after the police did. It's possible that he was there the whole time, though he claimed that he wasn't."

"Yes, he has all the hallmarks of a good suspect.

But he's not the only one." Tessa cracked the egg into the bowl. "Who's next?"

"There's Kelvin, he's a local who went to college with Sandy. He seemed to have a big bone to pick with her when he spoke about her at the diner." Cassie jotted Kelvin's name down on the list, then closed her eyes for a moment. "I'd say that anyone she worked with could be a suspect."

"You met a few of them, didn't you? Did you notice anything strange about any of them?" Tessa added some vanilla extract to the egg.

"Not really." Cassie frowned. "But Mirabel did mention that Craig might be in a relationship with Sandy."

"Oh, that definitely makes him a suspect!" Tessa poured some molasses into the butter. "Love that smell." A faint smile graced her lips.

"You're right, I hate to think he could do something like this, he was such a cute kid. But any kind of romantic relationship could be a reason for murder." Cassie rolled her eyes. "I can certainly see that now."

"Still no word from Sebastian?" Tessa raised an eyebrow.

"He has his own things to deal with." Cassie cleared her throat, then refocused on the list. "What about the assistant producer? If Nel demanded authenticity all the time, I'm guessing that she and Sandy butted heads now and then. Especially seeing as the budget for the show had been cut."

"I hate to agree with you on that, but you're right. Nel is smart as a whip, too, as far as I can tell." Tessa added in some brown sugar and beat the mixture together. "Maybe the murderer panicked."

Cassie added Nel's name to the list, then sat back in her chair and closed her eyes. She pictured the people from the show that she'd met. Lionel had been quite friendly. As one of the lead actors she guessed that he had a lot of interaction with Sandy.

"Lionel is a possibility, too, I suppose. He didn't seem to have any issues with Sandy, but we should dig a little deeper and see if there's something we don't know about." She scribbled his name down.

"It's good to have a list, but now we need a plan." Tessa walked over to another empty bowl and dumped some flour into it, followed by some baking soda. "Do you want to help me with the spices?"

"Sure." Cassie stepped up beside her.

"We need a bit of salt." Tessa nodded to the salt shaker.

"Who should we talk to first?" Cassie sprinkled the salt in.

"Next, the ginger, a big spoonful." Tessa sighed. "If it were me, I would speak to the person most likely to be the most thrown off by the death. If she and Craig really were in a relationship, he'd be the most emotionally raw. Even if he's the one who killed her, he'd still be reeling from the loss." She nodded. "That's enough ginger. Add in some of the nutmeg, and cloves."

"This much?" Cassie estimated what some meant.

"Perfect. Oh! The cinnamon! I can't believe I almost forgot the cinnamon!" Tessa grabbed a bottle from the cabinet and handed it to Cassie. "Can't have gingerbread cookies without the cinnamon."

"Is this enough?" Cassie glanced up at her.

"Just a dash more, then stir it up." Tessa handed Cassie a whisk.

"Do you think he'll even talk to us? How do we know he hasn't left town yet? I'm not sure where he's staying." Cassie whisked the ingredients together, then handed the bowl over to Tessa.

"I'm sure Oliver has instructed that he and the other actors and crew need to stay in town at the moment for the investigation. And I know where they're staying. The new inn just outside of town, by the creek. I'm guessing he will be willing to talk to you, you have some history. One thing about actors, is they tend to like attention." Tessa blended the dry ingredients into the wet mixture, then turned off the mixer. "We can go talk to him while the cookie dough chills. It'll be easier to cut out the gingerbread cookies the longer it chills." She divided the dough into two and wrapped it in plastic wrap.

"Thanks for doing this, Tessa." Cassie smiled at her as she set the dough in the fridge.

"Trust me, this town is going to need all the Christmas cheer it can get." Tessa frowned. "Once news breaks about this, we're going to be famous for the wrong reasons."

CHAPTER 8

"Do you really think any of them will talk to us now?" Cassie stared up at the inn Tessa parked in front of. "They've all just had such a shock, maybe we should wait."

"This is the best time to find out information. While people are still processing what happened, information is likely to be fresh in their minds, and they are less likely to lie." Tessa pointed to the plate of cookies that Cassie held in her lap. "Besides, we brought those to sweeten the pot. I wasn't too happy with how this batch turned out, but they still taste good. I tweaked the recipe a bit to make it my own."

"Let's give it a try." Cassie stepped out of the jeep and walked around to Tessa.

"There's Sasha, one of the owners." Tessa grabbed

Harry's leash and the dog leaped out of the car. "She has a few dogs and loves Harry. I'm going to see if I can find out anything from her. You go inside and get started. I'll meet you in there."

"Okay." Cassie's heart raced. She felt much more comfortable when Tessa was with her when trying to find out information.

Cassie carried the cookies into the lobby of the inn.

As Cassie had hoped, a few people were gathered in the sitting area near the fireplace. She set the plate of cookies down on a coffee table in the center of the room. As she straightened up, her elbow grazed the arm of someone who walked past her.

"Excuse me, sorry." Cassie took a step back as her eyes settled on Craig.

"Everything in this town is too small. Everyone's always bumping into each other." Craig huffed.

"Craig." Cassie pushed her curls back behind her ear and leaned closer to him. "I'm so sorry for your loss."

"My loss?" Craig cut his gaze in her direction. "What would you know about my loss?"

"I heard that you and Sandy spent quite a bit of time together." Cassie searched his eyes as he stared at her.

"What do you want?" Craig took a step back, though his eyes never left hers. "An autograph?"

"No thanks, I've never actually seen the show. But I'm sure that you are great in it." Cassie nudged the plate of cookies closer to him. "Have something to eat. I know when you lose someone, it's hard to eat anything at all, but it can help settle your emotions, if you at least eat something."

"You've lost someone?" Craig picked up one of the cookies and broke off a piece of it.

"Yes, I did lose someone. My husband. Michael. Remember, I saw you at the diner, I told you he worked for your dad." Cassie lowered her voice. "It was very difficult to lose him. It still is sometimes."

"Did it feel like your heart was ripped out and thrown onto the ground?" Craig pursed his lips. "Or did you not really love him?"

Cassie flinched as his comment hit a nerve. She hadn't really loved her husband but it still hurt when he passed away. He was a huge part of her life and she missed him. She forced herself to look back at Craig.

"Is that what it felt like for you? Because you were in love with Sandy?"

"Avoiding the question with a question." Craig chuckled, then sank down into a chair. "Yes, it's true.

The rumors are all true. Sandy and I were in love. We were going to spend the rest of our lives together."

"You were going to get married?" Cassie's eyes widened at the thought.

"I don't know about that. You don't have to get married these days you know. But we were going to be together." Craig frowned as he picked up another cookie. "That's all gone now." He snapped the cookie in half.

"I know this is hard for you, but what do you think happened to her?" Cassie sat down in the chair beside him. "Who would want to hurt her like this?"

"I think she finally pushed someone too far." Craig stared at the broken cookie in his hands. "I told her before, her meanness was going to get her hurt one of these days."

"Meanness? Did you think she was mean?" Cassie's fingertips itched for the pen and notebook in her purse.

"Of course she was. Anyone will tell you that. Nothing was more important than the work. No matter what was going on in her life, she always dropped everything to make sure her work got done. Sometimes she'd go days without sleeping to make sure a scene was right, which meant that the crew would go days without sleeping, too." Craig shrugged. "If people didn't like it, they didn't have to work with her."

"That seems a little extreme." Cassie frowned.

"It was passionate, that's what it was." Craig wiped a tear from his cheek. It appeared as if he really was upset by Sandy's murder. But was that because he was upset by losing her? Or upset because he had murdered her?

Cassie noticed a few cuts on his hand.

"Did you hurt yourself?" She tipped her head toward his hand.

"Sure did, on that overgrown property that Anton tricked Sandy into using for the episode. I was helping her try to figure out how we could still use the property as a setting, and got my hand scratched up by a sticker bush." Craig shook his head as he looked at the cuts. "Luckily, I don't think they got infected, though I'm surprised they didn't, considering the state of that place."

Cassie did her best to memorize the sight of the cuts. She intended to add them to her notebook later. He could be telling the truth, but he could also be covering up for wounds that he got while murdering Sandy.

"Sorry that happened." Cassie nodded. "She was

lucky to have you helping her out. Do you know why she was at the property so early, all alone?”

“She wasn’t alone.” Craig quirked an eyebrow.

“What do you mean? Were you there with her?”

“No, she was there with her killer.” Craig rolled his eyes. “Try to keep up.”

“I’m just trying to piece things together.” Cassie’s cheeks burned. She noticed Tessa standing at the front desk. She guessed that as a former detective Tessa would get a lot more information out of Craig than she was. “But if you two were always together, why wouldn’t she have told you that she was at the property early? Or who she was meeting with?”

“I don’t want to talk about this anymore.” Craig snatched up another cookie, then turned and stalked off toward the stairs.

“Ouch.” Tessa stepped up beside her. “It looks like that didn’t end well.”

“Tessa, you should have been here. I don’t think he’s ever going to talk to me again.” Cassie frowned.

“You were doing a great job, from what I could see. I knew that he would be more likely to talk to you, that’s why I hung back by the front desk.”

“Where’s Harry?” Cassie looked at Tessa.

“Out the back with Sasha’s dogs. He’s having a ball.” Tessa smiled. “I asked her about their security, and cameras. Unfortunately, they don't have much of either. It will be difficult to tell who came and went from here this morning. Did you find out anything at all from Craig?"

"Only that apparently he was in love with Sandy. He claimed they were going to be together forever. But when I mentioned marriage, he was very dismissive. Also, when I pointed out that he didn't know who she was with this morning, he ended the conversation." Cassie looked toward the stairs. "I think I might have lost any chance we had of getting any information out of him."

"Oh, but you hit a gold mine." Tessa wrapped her arm around Cassie's and led her to the door. "You found out that things were not as good between Craig and Sandy as he claimed. He's grieving sure, but he's also jealous, and hurt. He doesn't know who she was with, and that makes him feel a little betrayed. Or maybe, he's just trying to put on a show to cover up his own guilt and he was with her. Either way, we know that he's still a good suspect, especially with that temper."

"Interesting." Cassie nodded. Had he interrupted a secret tryst? "If she was cheating on him, maybe he caught her. But why wouldn't the other man have come forward by now about it?"

"Maybe he waited until he was gone, or maybe the other man has reasons to keep their relationship a secret. Either way, it's just a theory right now. I have another one we need to follow up on. According to Sasha, she had to get her son to kick Kelvin out of the lobby last night. He showed up here, eager to confront Sandy. I think we need to consider him a high priority suspect at the moment. I think we need to try catch up with him."

"And, I just happen to know where he'll be."

"You do? Where?" Tessa narrowed her eyes.

"At the diner. He comes in for lunch at eleven thirty almost every day." Cassie smiled.

"Want to check it out?" Tessa walked toward the garden at the back. She was just about to call Harry when he bounded toward them.

"Oh no." Cassie gasped. Harry was covered in mud. Before Cassie or Tessa could stop him, he jumped up, put his paws on Cassie's stomach and licked her cheek. Covering her face, jeans, arms and t-shirt in mud. She winced and tried to turn her head away.

"Harry down!" The command wasn't very stern as Tessa was laughing, but Harry obeyed.

"I'm so sorry." A woman who looked to be in her sixties with short, brown hair came running up to them. "I opened the gate and before I could stop them Jumper and Harry went straight for the mud by the creek. That Golden Retriever would be covered in it all the time if he could."

"That's okay, Sasha." Tessa laughed.

Cassie laughed as well as she tried to wipe the mud off of her face. Tessa introduced her to Sasha.

"Why don't you leave Harry here and I'll get him washed up for you." Sasha smiled. "We can't let him get into your jeep like that. You can pick him up later when he's dried off." She looked at Cassie. "I'll get you a towel."

"Thanks." Cassie wiped her cheek with her hand.

They all followed Sasha to the backyard.

"Harry, you cheeky pup." Tessa tried to sound stern, but there was a hint of amusement in her voice. Harry barked at the sound of his name, apparently oblivious to the mess he'd made.

After Cassie had wiped off as much mud as she could, they left Harry at the inn to get cleaned up and dried off. Then they headed back to the jeep.

"Let's go home and you can change." Tessa started the jeep. "Then we can head to the diner to see if Kelvin is still there. It's a bit early for lunch. But I could handle a milkshake."

"Yes, let's do that. Hopefully, we aren't too late to

catch him there." Cassie pulled her notebook out of her purse as she settled in the passenger seat. While she outlined what she could remember from her conversation with Craig, she told Tessa about the cuts she'd seen.

"It's very possible that he got them exactly as he said he did, but we'll make sure to feed Oliver that tidbit of information. Maybe he doesn't have it yet."

CHAPTER 9

After Cassie got changed, Tessa drove the short distance to the diner, and parked out front.

They stepped out of the jeep and headed through the door of the diner.

"Hi Cassie." Tamera walked over to her. Her eyes widened at the sight of Tessa. Tessa preferred to keep to herself and didn't often come into the diner. "Tessa." She smiled, then looked back at Cassie. "You aren't working today, are you?"

"No, we just wanted to grab a milkshake." Cassie glanced over and saw Kelvin at his usual spot at a table in the corner.

"Great, it's pretty busy." Tamera looked around.

"Where's Sebastian? I'm used to the two of you coming in together."

"Not sure." Cassie shrugged and hoped that her expression remained steady.

"Is the counter okay?" Tamera gestured toward the counter. The rest of the tables were full.

"I might see if Kelvin wants company." Cassie looked toward Kelvin's table.

"Sure." Tamera glanced over at Kelvin. "Holler when you're ready to order."

"I actually just want a chocolate milkshake." Cassie smiled.

"Caramel for me." Tessa nodded.

"I don't know how you can drink a milkshake in this weather." Tamera shivered, then walked toward the counter.

Cassie walked over to Kelvin's table with Tessa close behind and paused beside it.

"Do you mind if we sit?"

"I was hoping for a little quiet. I was hoping to keep to myself and avoid the crowds." Kelvin looked up at them, then sighed and nodded. "Fine, sit if you like."

"Thanks so much." Cassie settled in the chair beside him and Tessa took the chair beside her. "Do you always try to avoid the crowds?"

"No, I just didn't want to hear the same story over and over again. Sandy's death is going to be on everyone's mind, and I don't want to be in the middle of it." Kelvin had the last bite of his burger. Cassie knew she wouldn't have much time to talk to him if he had already finished eating. "But somehow I'm guessing that's why you're talking to me. Since, you were the one that found her."

"You heard about that already?" Cassie raised an eyebrow. "Word gets around fast."

"In a town like this, it sure does." Kelvin pursed his lips, then sat back in his chair. "I guess you're trying to find out what happened, like you always do."

"Yes." Cassie tried to hide her shock at the realization that he knew that she liked to do some investigating of her own. "After finding her, I really want to know why it happened. I'd like to know more about her." She narrowed her eyes. "It's strange to have someone you know nothing about die in the town where you live, you know? She was here so briefly. I just wish I had some kind of idea of who she was. I remember you saying that you knew Sandy in college?" She scooted her chair closer to his. "Why don't you tell me more about what she was like then?"

"What she was like?" Kelvin laughed, then tightened his lips. "She was terrible. I guess karma finally caught up with her."

"I'm sure there are a few more specific details that you can share with me." Cassie's tone hardened as she settled her gaze on him. "We are talking about a murder here."

"I get it." Kelvin cleared his throat. "Sure, I wouldn't have wished anyone to be murdered. But if she walked into it, she walked into it. As far as details, well, to be clearer, she was absolutely horrendous. She honed in on me on the first day of class. She wanted me to give her the answers on a test, then she wanted me to do her homework. When I refused, she orchestrated a ridiculous ruse that painted me as a cheater, and a fraud. I'd spent years earning my way into that school, and in one week she took everything from me."

"Really? How could one woman wreak that kind of havoc?" Cassie held his gaze. "Are you sure there wasn't any truth to her allegations?"

"Not a shred of truth." Kelvin shook his head. "Up until that point in my life I had lived with extreme authenticity and honesty, and what did it get me? She targeted me and wouldn't stop until she ground me into dust. So no, I don't feel any sympathy for her. If she hadn't been such a horrible person, she likely wouldn't have ended up dead."

"You do realize that talking like that doesn't exactly make you sound innocent?" Cassie met his eyes.

"Suspect me all you want. I didn't do it." Kelvin's eyes grew stern as he stared back at her. "I'm not going to let her ruin my life for a second time, you can believe that."

The conversation stopped as Tamera brought them their milkshakes.

"Thank you." Tessa and Cassie looked up at her in unison. Cassie looked back at Kelvin as Tamera walked away.

"Well, if you have an alibi, you won't have to worry about that." Cassie raised an eyebrow. "Did you give the police your alibi?"

"I didn't say a word to the police, and I won't be." Kelvin swung around and pointed a finger at Tessa as he continued. "And I don't have to say a word to you, either."

"Of course you don't, Kelvin." Tessa smiled. "We're both on your side, alright? You say you didn't have anything to do with Sandy's murder, and I believe you. But the only way to clear your name is if you are honest. Let us help you figure this out. I'm not interested in making your life harder, I want to make sure that the guilty party gets caught. So, where were you?"

Kelvin sighed and let his hand fall back to his side.

"I was at home, sleeping. Where else would I be? It was early in the morning. I don't go into work until the afternoon, after I have lunch here. Before you ask, no, no one can back me up on that. You know I live alone, and I doubt that my neighbors have any interest in me. So, I guess that means you can't cross me off your list?" Kelvin rolled his eyes. "Just because I'm a loner, that doesn't make me a killer."

"I don't think it does. I also prefer to keep to myself most of the time. You know I live alone, too, Kelvin. I prefer it that way." Tessa smiled at him. "Try not to worry too much, this will get sorted out."

As Tessa and Cassie walked out of the diner, Cassie turned toward her.

"That didn't go so well, did it?"

"Not the way I wanted it to. I had hoped that he would implicate himself, and in some ways he did. There's no doubt that he hated Sandy, and still held a grudge from their time in college together. He also doesn't have a solid alibi. But that doesn't make him a killer." Tessa frowned as she glanced back toward the diner. "I don't know, I just don't think he would spend so much time talking to us about it if he actually did it."

"Unless." Cassie pulled open the door of the jeep.

"Unless what?" Tessa sat down in the driver's seat.

"Unless, he's just lonely enough to want attention anyway he can get it. Maybe he's hoping to get caught." Cassie met her eyes. "Maybe he got his revenge, and he wants people to notice that he took charge. It might seem twisted, but killing Sandy might not have been enough for him. He may need the rest of the world to know that he did it."

"That is definitely a possibility." Tessa frowned. "I think it's time we spoke to someone who probably knows everything about what goes on behind the scenes of Inspector Heathcliffe. Lionel!"

"So, Lionel is the only one not staying at the inn?" Cassie looked up from her phone and frowned. "I wonder why that is?"

"He and his brother have an RV they travel around in." Tessa shrugged. "I did a little research on him, and it seems he keeps himself pretty separated from the rest of the crew."

"He plays the partner of the main detective on the show, right?" Cassie looked back down at her phone. "Charles Cayata plays Inspector Heathcliffe?"

"Yes, that's right." Tessa headed toward the inn. "I just want to pick up Harry on the way, before he lands up in the mud again."

"Good idea." Cassie laughed.

Tessa turned down the road to the inn.

"It looks like the police are here." Cassie pointed through the windshield at the police cars.

"Must be doing another round of questioning." Tessa parked the jeep. "I'll just quickly get Harry."

Cassie got out of the jeep as well. She needed some fresh air. A few minutes later, Harry bounded around the corner and straight for her. She instinctively cringed, hoping he wasn't covered in mud, again. But as he got closer she could see that he was completely clean.

"Hi buddy." She crouched down to rub behind his ears and he licked her cheeks. "You look so clean."

Cassie opened the back door of the jeep and Harry jumped in.

Tessa got in on the driver's side.

"Well, Harry's all cleaned up at least." Tessa smiled. "You cheeky pup."

Harry barked in response as if he was agreeing with Tessa.

"Hopefully, Lionel is still there." Tessa started the jeep.

"So, where is Charles? If everyone else is here to record the episode, then why isn't the star of the show here?" Cassie looked back down at the picture of the cast on her screen.

"Apparently, he isn't in most of this episode. The

plot line focuses around his abduction, his team is working to rescue him, and his scenes don't come in until the very end of the episode. I guess he planned to arrive later, and now that there's been a murder, from what Oliver told me, he's not planning on getting anywhere near Little Leaf Creek until the murderer is in custody." Tessa turned down the road that led to the local campground.

"You talked to Oliver?" Cassie tucked her phone into her purse.

"Yes, he wanted to check in after we sent him that information earlier. I was surprised he called me instead of you." Tessa smiled some as she pulled up beside a large RV and put the jeep in park.

"Progress." Cassie winked at her. "I love it."

"It was just a phone call, Cassie." Tessa stepped out of the jeep. "We still have a long road ahead of us, to get back to where we were."

"Maybe you don't have to go back." Cassie met her eyes as they reached the side of the RV. "Maybe, like you told me about celebrating Christmas my way, you can start somewhere new."

"I like that." Tessa smiled, then gave a firm knock on the RV door.

The door to the RV popped open and a man poked his head out.

"Yeah?" He looked between the two women.

"We're here to speak with Lionel." Cassie met his eyes. "You're his brother, Simon, right?"

"Brother, manager, friend." Simon nodded as he looked between them again. "This isn't the best time to ask for autographs."

"We're not here for an autograph." Tessa shook her head. "We just wanted to speak to Lionel."

"Are you cops?" Simon eyed Tessa as he took a slight step back. "We already spoke to the police today."

"No, we're not cops." Cassie wrapped her hand around the door to prevent him from closing it.

"We just want to chat with him. See if we can help him." Tessa smiled. Harry stepped out from behind Tessa.

"Oh, I didn't see you there." Simon's eyes lit up as he bent down and held out his hand for Harry to sniff. "Aren't you a cutey." He looked back up at Tessa. "Help him how?" He narrowed his eyes. "I doubt that he needs any help from you." He glared at Tessa as he patted Harry's head.

"Really? Because if it is revealed that he is one of the main suspects in a murder investigation, even if he isn't the murderer, it's going to lead to trouble. I'm sure you're already aware people love a scandal more than they love the truth. When word gets out that Lionel is suspected of killing Sandy, it'll be all over the newspapers and magazines."

"And the internet." Cassie glanced at Tessa. "If it's not there already. Even if the police can't prove that it was Lionel that killed Sandy, he's going to get a ton of terrible publicity."

"And how exactly do you plan to help with that?" Simon settled his gaze on Cassie. "Are you a reporter? Or let me guess, some kind of entertainment blogger? You were just posing as a waitress, right?"

"No." Cassie stared into his eyes. "We just want the real killer caught, and fast, so that the scandal can be put to rest before it even gets started. This is our town, and we want it back to normal as quickly as possible."

"Who is there?" A voice came from behind Simon.

"Some ladies, want to speak to you." Simon glanced back into the trailer, then looked back at Cassie. "Just give me a second."

Cassie stepped back as he closed the door.

A few minutes later the door opened and Lionel stepped out of the trailer, dressed in a t-shirt and shorts. He shivered as an icy breeze ruffled his hair.

"Don't you want to put something warmer on?" Cassie frowned.

"Look." Lionel held out his arms and hands, then slowly spun around. "See? Not a single mark. Not a bruise on me." He turned back to face them both again. "I can tell you right now, if I had attacked Sandy it would be obvious. She's trained in martial arts, did you know that?"

"No, I didn't know that." Cassie held up a hand. "Lionel, it's okay, just relax. We're not here to accuse you of anything."

"I'm sorry." Lionel sighed. "I'm just really shocked by all of this. The police grilled me earlier today, and I'm still processing what happened to Sandy. I still can't wrap my head around the idea that she's really gone. I've been trying to reach Nel, and she's not answering her phone. I have no idea what happens from here. So, you two showing up with more questions, I just don't want to deal with it."

Lionel didn't even seem to notice Harry. Cassie guessed that unlike his brother he wasn't much of a dog lover, or maybe he was just distracted by everything going on.

"We don't mean to cause you more stress." Cassie's tone softened as she noticed the quake in his voice. "I spoke to Craig earlier, and he mentioned their relationship. I'm sure that you were all very close to Sandy. I'm sorry for your loss."

"Craig's relationship?" A short laugh erupted from Lionel's lips. "Is that what he called it?"

"He said they were very much in love." Tessa cleared her throat. "Is that inaccurate?"

"Quite. It would take a huge leap of the imagination to characterize their connection as any kind of relationship, let alone love." Lionel wiped his hand across his face. "Craig was obsessed, and Sandy had finally had enough. He was furious when she broke things off."

"Broke things off?" Cassie's heart skipped a beat, she glanced at Tessa, then looked back at Lionel. "Are you saying that Sandy broke up with him recently?"

"No, I'm saying that Sandy wanted a bit of fun. She didn't want to be tied down. Craig was looking for something more serious. They had a bit of a fight, as soon as we arrived here." Lionel lowered his voice. "It's not my business to judge. Craig just wouldn't get it through his head that she didn't have any real feelings for him, she just wanted a bit of fun."

"And you." Cassie looked over at Lionel. "Did you and Sandy ever date?"

"No." Lionel stared hard into her eyes for a moment. "Look, I've got nothing more to say about this. I had nothing to do with Sandy's murder. I don't want to talk about this anymore." He grabbed the door and pulled it shut.

CHAPTER 11

"Ouch." Tessa stared at the door. "I think you hit a sore spot."

"Do you think they really had a relationship?" Cassie followed her to the jeep. "Maybe I shouldn't have said that. I feel like I'm just causing people to shut us out." She sighed. "You should really do the talking."

"You're doing great, Cassie." Tessa popped Harry in the back of the jeep, then settled inside. "It wouldn't have even crossed my mind to make that connection at the moment. Which makes me wonder, why did you think of it so quickly?"

"I don't know." Cassie shoved her seat belt into the latch, then stared out through the windshield.

"Still nothing from Sebastian?" Tessa started the jeep.

"It's worse than that." Cassie sighed. "I'm sure you'll think it's silly."

"Why do you say that?" Tessa drove down the road, away from the campground.

"You don't seem like the type of person to be thrown off by anything, especially romance." Cassie shook her head. "I'm trying not to let it distract me, but I just don't know what to think anymore."

"Cassie, we're friends, aren't we?" Tessa patted her hand. "You can tell me anything. I want you to. As for my experience with romance, I wasn't always an old lady, you know." She chuckled, but the laughter sounded awkward.

"Thanks Tessa." Cassie leaned her head back against the seat and closed her eyes. "I think, I think he's seeing someone else. Actually, I don't just think that. I know that."

"Sebastian?" Tessa looked over at her. "Without telling you?"

"It's not like we've officially declared that we are in a relationship, I guess." Cassie fiddled with the zipper on her purse. "I thought we had something, but my experience with romance starts and ends with my late husband. Honestly, I had no idea what I was getting into with Sebastian. I understand if he wants to move on, but it would have been nice if he'd at least told me."

"Listen Cassie, I'm not one to meddle, but I have known Sebastian quite a bit longer than you. Yes, he's dated around a good amount, as a handsome young man like him should. But I've never known him to be dishonest. Even if he had lost interest, I'm sure he would have told you. Maybe you're mistaken?"

"Maybe." Cassie released a heavy breath. "But I don't think so. Where are we going?"

"Time for coffee." Tessa pulled into the local coffee shop and parked. "Would you mind going in for me? I think I've had enough socializing today and I can keep Harry company."

Harry barked in response.

"Sure, no problem." Cassie eagerly left the jeep. She knew that Tessa meant well, but she doubted her assertion that she was mistaken about Sebastian's behavior. She couldn't think of a single explanation for him spending time with another woman, while not even bothering to explain it to her. A quick check of her phone confirmed yet again that she hadn't heard anything from him. Maybe that was the reason she had accused Lionel of being jealous over Craig's relationship with Sandy.

Cassie stepped into the coffee shop and walked up to the front counter. With a few people ahead of her, she needed something to distract her from her thoughts, which swirled between homicide and heartbreak. She plucked a small booklet from a glass display beside the register and began to thumb through it. By the time she reached the front of the line she'd read through several dark, but meaningful poems.

"Are you buying that?" The barista smiled as she pointed at the book.

"Yes, I'd like to. It's by a local author?"

"Yup." She tipped her head toward a table near the back of the shop. "She's right over there, actually. She'll be thrilled someone bought a copy. Poor thing has been so upset since her writing for Inspector Heathcliffe got rejected. She wrote an entire episode. But this will brighten her day."

Cassie glanced at the name on the book she held as she handed over her payment to the barista.

"Well, maybe I'll just stop by to tell her how much I enjoy it while I wait for my coffees." Cassie smiled as she walked over to the author's table. "Heather?"

She pulled out the chair beside her. "Do you mind if I sit down for a moment?"

"There are plenty of empty tables." Heather didn't look up from the blank page in the notebook in front of her.

"I understand." Cassie settled in the chair and lowered her voice. "But I actually wanted to talk to you."

"Me?" Heather glanced up from the notebook. "Why?" Her eyes narrowed.

"I read some of your poetry just now." Cassie held up the booklet she'd purchased. "It is beautiful." She smiled as she met her eyes. "I just wanted to meet the person who wrote it."

"Meet me?" Heather gave a short laugh. "We've been introduced a few times. But I wouldn't expect the new woman in town to notice someone like me. I've lived here all my life, and more people know your name, than will ever know my name."

"Oh, Heather, I don't believe that. Not with your kind of talent." Cassie searched her memory for any time she'd met Heather before. Was she telling the truth? She couldn't remember ever meeting her. Maybe she had served her at the diner. But everyone was new to her in Little Leaf Creek, and it was difficult to remember all of them. "I'm sorry if I've overlooked you. My move here was a little rough, and I've been pretty preoccupied. I'm glad to have met you now."

"Did you really like my poems?" Heather sat back in her chair as she studied Cassie. "Or, are you just trying to get something from me?"

"I'm not trying to get anything from you." Cassie smiled. "I did like your poems. I think they're beautiful, and also thought-provoking."

"But that's not the only reason that you're here." Heather frowned as she looked back at her notebook. "It's not like you're interrupting anything. I can't write a single word, since Sandy—"

"Since Sandy was murdered?" Cassie nodded. "It's been shocking for everyone."

"You know what's funny?" Heather looked up at her, then sighed.

"What?" Cassie searched her expression for any sign of what she might say.

"I was so nervous all day today. I even packed a bag." Heather shook her head as she rolled her eyes. "I was just absolutely certain that the police would show up at my door and accuse me of killing Sandy. I mean, I did ask her to read the episode I wrote for the show, and she did reject it, without even bothering to read it. She was awful and rude. Of course, that would make me a suspect, right?"

Cassie's eyes widened.

"Maybe?"

"It would at least make me someone they would want to speak to, right?" Heather smirked, then looked up at the ceiling. "But no. That knock never came. No phone call, either. Because even when someone is murdered, I don't exist. Not to the police, not to this town." She tilted her head to the side as she regarded Cassie. "So, why do I all of a sudden exist to you, Cassie? What's sparked your interest? Don't try to con me. I know it wasn't my poetry."

"I do like your poetry." Cassie smiled. "But I did also hear about Sandy rejecting your work. You might have been one of the last people to see her alive. So, it did make me curious about what the two of you might have talked about."

"Sure it did." Heather sighed as her shoulders slumped. "As I planned to tell the police, who never showed up, we didn't talk about anything. I found out she would be out at Anton's property, so I decided to take a huge leap of faith. She'd refused to meet with me when I tried to make an appointment, so I thought if I just showed up maybe she'd spare me a minute. But when I got there last night, she laughed in my face. She told me to leave before she called the police on me. She didn't even look at my work." She tapped her pen against the paper in front of her. "So, back to the beginning for me, right? Trust me, Cassie, I may enjoy writing murder mysteries, but I would never be an interesting enough person to even think about committing one."

Cassie stared into her eyes in an attempt to see past her self-loathing, and the bitterness she carried. Could there be a murderer lurking beneath that low self-esteem?

CHAPTER 12

Cassie walked back out to the jeep with two hot coffees in her hands.

Tessa popped open the door for her as she pulled her phone away from her ear.

As she handed Tessa her coffee, Cassie noticed her slip her phone into her pocket.

"Ollie?"

"No." Tessa blew into the opening. "Thanks for the coffee."

Harry popped his head between the seats and licked Cassie's cheek. She rubbed behind his ears with her free hand.

"That's not all I brought you." Cassie filled her in on her conversation with Heather. "She saw Sandy last night. I think it's possible she brewed all night over the rejection, then decided to do something about it early this morning."

"Rejection is a hard thing to swallow." Tessa tapped the side of her coffee cup. "But Heather isn't the only one who was rejected, right?"

"Do you mean Craig? If Lionel is telling the truth, then Sandy broke up with him." Cassie nodded.

"That's true, but I mean Anton. He worked hard to get Sandy to come here and use his parents' property for the episode. What if she changed her mind about using it? We already know that she was very unhappy about the state of the property when she saw it."

"He is the one person we absolutely know that she had a problem with as soon as she arrived in town. And since he has roots here, he might have felt more comfortable taking action against her." Cassie shook her head.

"I think we should take a drive out to the property. According to an old colleague of mine, Anton is out there demanding that the crime scene be released." Tessa rolled her eyes as she started the jeep.

"Really? Why would he be doing that." Cassie took a small sip of her hot coffee.

"I guess Anton is trying to insist that his parents

be allowed back home, but Oliver has refused to release the crime scene because it is still being processed and he hasn't been able to determine where the actual murder took place just yet. Anton's parents gave Sandy and the crew access to the house during filming. Oliver believes that Sandy was killed somewhere else and her body was moved to the shed, in an attempt to make it harder to find. Or maybe in an attempt to make the murder harder to solve." Tessa glanced over at her. "Probably by someone who knew where to move the body. Anton may be trying to hurry them off the property because he's afraid they'll find more evidence against him."

"That would make sense." Cassie stepped out of the jeep and opened the door for Harry.

"Especially, if the killer knew they only had a short time before the crew would arrive. It sounds like the killer hadn't planned ahead very well, so this could have been a spur of the moment crime of passion."

"Maybe." Cassie met Tessa's eyes. "Anton is a possibility, but what about Craig?"

"I'm thinking he's definitely a possibility. But the only person to arrive quickly to the crime scene was Anton. He claimed he had a meeting with Sandy, but what if that was just a cover up for why he was on the scene?" Tessa raised an eyebrow as she took Harry's leash from Cassie. "Just because he pulled up, doesn't mean that he came off the road. Maybe his car was parked somewhere else on the property."

"Good thinking!" Cassie snapped her fingers. "I'm sure that he thought pulling up to the crime scene would look better than driving away from it."

"It looks like he's already here." Tessa tipped her head toward a car parked near the house. Beside it was another car, both had California license plates. "He must be meeting with someone from the show."

"The door to the house is open." Cassie pointed to the sliver of light showing through the door. "Should we go up and knock?"

"Maybe we should see what we can find out before we alert them to our presence." Tessa walked toward a window not far from the front porch. "Let's see what we can hear."

Cassie leaned close to the window, which had a few cracks and gaps around the frame.

"I just want to know the truth!" A voice shouted inside. Cassie could see that it was Nel.

"And you think I don't?" Anton's voice raised. "This happened on my family's land! My parents can't even come home. They are so upset. All I can tell them is that I don't have any answers. Don't you think I want to know the truth more than anyone?" The floorboard creaked as he stepped forward. "And by the way, I don't appreciate you assuming that I had something to do with Sandy's murder. You of all people should have more loyalty toward me than that."

"Anton, that's why I'm here. I wanted to ask you face to face. I know that you've done a lot for me in the past. But I also know that Sandy was furious with you over all of this. I know that the two of you fought yesterday. How can I not be concerned that you had something to do with this? Maybe she pushed you too far." Nel sighed as her voice softened. "Anton, I wouldn't exactly blame you."

"Wow." Anton shook his head, then cleared his throat. "You know I'm not the only one that could be implicated in this. You had as much reason to want to get rid of Sandy as me."

"What are you talking about?" Nel gasped.

"I'm talking about the fact that Sandy wanted to fire you, Nel. I've been trying to convince her not to, and so have a few other people. But you were top on her list to get rid of, because you increased production costs so much by insisting that things always be true to life. With the budget cutbacks things have become even more tight, we can't even afford security anymore. Sandy was worried there wouldn't be enough money to film the show. She also felt threatened by you." Anton crossed his arms as he stared at her. "You know as well as I do, that she didn't appreciate the effort you put in. Maybe she decided this was the right time to let you go. Maybe you didn't want to lose your job, and saw killing her as the only way to avoid it."

"Unbelievable!" Nel threw her hands in the air. "I would never do something like that! I wouldn't even really know how to kill anyone!"

"Is that the argument you're going to tell the police? Do you think they will believe you when you make every murder on the show as authentic as possible?" Anton chuckled. "No one is going to believe that you don't know how to kill someone."

"That's different." Nel glared at him. "It's research. Not real life. I would never hurt anyone."

"It's always the quiet ones." Anton shook his head.

"How could you even accuse me of this?" Nel's voice trembled.

Cassie peered through the glass and noticed tears flowing down Nel's cheeks.

"The same way that you accused me, Nel. The

same way that you came here, and looked into my eyes, and really thought that I could have done something like this. I'm not a murderer."

"I never said you were." Nel shuddered as she turned away from him. "I just want to know what happened." She froze as her eyes locked to Cassie's through the window. "It looks like we have company."

"What are you doing there?" Anton shouted at the window as he stormed toward the front door.

"Think quick, Cassie." Tessa steered her and Harry away from the window. "Things are about to get very dicey."

Cassie held her breath as Anton made his way down off the porch.

"Anton, I can explain." She spit the words out, but had no idea how she would explain. Then she remembered they had left food there for the officers. "We just wanted to pick up the food containers from Mirabel's that we left for the officers, but it looks like it's all been taken care of."

"You need to leave." Anton stormed right past her, into the driveway, as Oliver's car pulled to a stop.

"No one should be in that house!" Oliver shouted out the open window at Anton, then jumped out of the car. "I told you, this entire property is a crime scene!"

Cassie noticed that Harry wagged his tail at the sight of Oliver. He strained on his leash as he tried to reach him. They had grown close to each other, before Tessa and Oliver had their disagreement. Cassie noticed that Oliver's eyes lit up slightly when he saw Harry, but darkened again when he looked back at Anton.

Cassie's attention was drawn toward the driveway to where a police car pulled up behind Oliver's car and an officer stepped out. Cassie recognized him as Patrick. The first officer that had arrived at the scene when she and Mirabel found Sandy's body. Another police car pulled up behind Patrick's car.

"I have every right to be here, this is my family's property!" Anton scowled at Oliver. Harry growled at Anton. "You have my parents terrified to come back here."

"I can't understand why you would want them to come back here, knowing what happened here." Oliver shook his head. "What if the killer comes back? Don't you want the killer caught before they return."

"Oh, the killer decided to take out Sandy and

then come back for my elderly parents?" Anton rolled his eyes. "No, I don't think so. You and I both know that Sandy was targeted, my parents aren't in any danger by being here. Nothing happened inside their house, there's no reason for you to keep them out."

"You say that as if you know for certain. But she did have access to the house, you know that, you gave it to her." Oliver crossed his arms, his eyes narrowed as he stared at Anton. "Since you have no alibi for the time that Sandy was killed, maybe it's time we had this discussion down at the station."

"Fine by me." Anton took a step closer to him. Harry growled at him and Anton took a step back. Harry was obviously protective of Oliver. "You don't have a single thing on me, and you know it. If you did, you'd already have me behind bars. It must be fun for you, having something to do for once, having a murder to investigate? You need to stop focusing all of your energy on me and my family instead of doing your job and finding the real killer."

CHAPTER 13

Cassie grabbed onto Tessa's arm as she watched Oliver's cheeks redden. She knew he had a temper, and she guessed that Anton was plucking his nerves.

"I will find out who killed Sandy, Anton. Whether it was you, or someone else, doesn't matter to me. All that matters is getting justice for the victim. You don't seem to want to help me with that. You worked with this woman for years, and her murder and finding her killer doesn't concern you?" Oliver crossed the remaining distance between himself and Anton. "I came out here, because someone called me out here. Someone who didn't feel safe."

"Are you kidding me?" Anton spun around to face Nel. "You called the police on me?"

"You were screaming at me." Nel wrapped her arms around herself as she shook her head. "I didn't know what you might do."

"Unbelievable!" Anton took a step toward her, but before he could complete it, Oliver had his hands pinned behind his back. Patrick stepped forward as well.

"I am going to take you down to the station." Oliver clasped handcuffs on Anton's wrists. "I just want to question you."

"I can't believe this is happening, I just can't believe it." Anton scowled.

As Oliver got him into the back of the car, Cassie looked over at Nel.

"Nel? Are you okay?"

"I am now." Nel sighed, then rubbed her hand along her arm. "He was losing it, you know? I just didn't know what to expect."

"You did the right thing." Tessa narrowed her eyes. "You can never be too careful."

Although Tessa's words delivered one message, her tone conveyed another. At least to Cassie it did. Tessa wasn't convinced of Nel's story.

"Cassie and Tessa, meet me down at the station so I can take your statements." Oliver looked over at them.

"I need to get Harry back home." Tessa looked at Oliver. "Is it okay if I give it to you later?" Cassie was surprised at how polite Tessa was.

"You can give it to Mick." Oliver gestured to the other police officer. Oliver's gaze skipped briefly over Tessa, before he focused on Nel. "I'll also need you to give a statement to Mick. Tell him every detail, alright?"

"Yes." Nel clasped her hands together and nodded. "I will."

"Patrick, I'll meet you at the station." Oliver nodded, then tossed a couple of treats to Harry who jumped up and caught them midair.

Oliver shot one more look in Cassie's direction, then got into the driver's seat of his car.

Patrick spoke to the other officer, then walked toward his patrol car.

"Maybe you should go talk to Oliver at the station. Maybe Patrick can give you a lift." Tessa nudged her. "You might find out something and I can see if Nel will tell me anything."

"Good idea." Cassie walked over to Patrick's car

just as he was about to close the door. "Mind if I get a ride with you down to the station?" She met his eyes as he looked at her.

"Sure, get in." Patrick started the car.

On the way to the police station, Cassie tried to get information about the murder from Patrick. Either he didn't have any or he didn't want to share it with her, because she found out nothing from him. Hopefully, she would be able to find out something at the station.

As Cassie opened the door to the station, she saw Oliver and Anton in the lobby.

"This is ridiculous, you need to let me go." Anton raised his voice. "Why am I under arrest when Nel was the one that was trespassing on my property? What about Cassie and Tessa, they were there as well?"

"You're not under arrest. I have just brought you into custody for questioning. While I have absolutely no idea why Cassie and Tessa were at your property, I didn't receive a complaint about them." Oliver steered him toward the back. "However, I did get a complaint about you, Anton."

"A complaint." Anton shouted. "I didn't do anything wrong."

"Anton, you need to relax." Oliver looked over at him. "You're just making things worse by acting like this."

"It's no act." Anton shook his head. "I've been trying to tell the police this from the start. I had nothing to do with her murder."

"And that is all you will say." Oliver walked him toward the back. "Maybe if you would give us something, anything to work with, then I wouldn't have to be wasting my time on dealing with you." He looked over at Cassie. "Meet me in my office. You can grab a coffee if you want." He pointed to the coffee station at the back. "I need to get Anton organized."

"Alright." Cassie nodded, then walked toward the back of the station.

She poured herself a cup of coffee and carried it into Oliver's office to wait for him. As she blew across the surface of the liquid, her thoughts traveled back to the argument between Anton and Nel. Was she really frightened of him, or had she called the police for another reason? Sure, it seemed Anton had a temper, but that didn't necessarily mean he was prone to violence. Did Nel know something more about Anton? She guessed they had worked side by side on the show. If she suspected him of killing Sandy, could she be right? She recalled Anton's description of Nel's tenuous work situation. Had Sandy really wanted to get rid of Nel? Would that be enough motivation to make her want to murder Sandy?

"Deep in thought, I see." Oliver stepped into his office. Cassie was so lost in thought that she jumped. She spilt some coffee on her hand and her top. "Sorry, I didn't mean to startle you. Are you okay?" He handed her a tissue.

"I'm ok." Cassie wiped her hands. "I was just distracted."

Oliver dropped down into the chair behind his desk.

"Maybe you've been thinking about why you were out at my crime scene?"

"We were just there to take a quick look around, we wanted to pick up the catering equipment." Cassie shrugged. "We didn't expect to stumble on that fight."

"How bad was it?" Oliver flipped open a file on his desk.

"They were shouting, but I'm not so sure that Anton would have done anything to hurt Nel." Cassie shook her head. "Of course, I can't be certain."

"That seems to be the case in every aspect of this crime." Oliver rubbed his hand across his forehead. "Questions leading to more questions."

"What have you found out?" Cassie took a sip of her coffee.

"That Sandy had a lot of people that didn't like her."

"I know you suspect that Anton might be involved. But what about Nel?" Cassie met his eyes. "They were arguing about Sandy being upset with her, I think Anton was accusing her of killing Sandy to protect her job."

"Interesting. I am aware there were some problems between Sandy and Nel. According to several of their associates, the friction had only been increasing lately. Sandy had the power to fire Nel if she wanted to, so there is a good chance that Nel felt pretty threatened by that." Oliver looked up as someone knocked on the open door. Cassie turned toward the door to see an officer standing there.

"Sorry to interrupt, I found something I want you to see on my computer when you're ready."

"That's okay." Oliver nodded to Cassie. "We were just finishing up. I'll come over in a second."

Oliver looked at Cassie.

"I have lots of work to do, Cassie. You need to be careful, you need to stay out of this."

"Of course." Cassie smiled as she looked into his eyes. "You know I'll be fine, especially when Tessa is with me."

"That's what I'm worried about. She knows how to get herself into trouble." Oliver stood up from his desk. "And not always how to get out of it."

"We'll be okay, don't worry." Cassie smiled.

"I'd better go see what he has to show me." Oliver walked through the door with Cassie behind him, then pointed toward the back of the station. "You can wash the coffee off over there."

"Thanks." Cassie blushed slightly at her clumsiness as she walked toward the back.

After Cassie had finished washing up, she started toward the front of the police station, when she heard Oliver's voice.

"That looks like a good lead."

Cassie instinctively hid around the corner. She peeked around the corner and saw the officer and Oliver hunched over a computer screen. They both looked at the screen.

"Yes, I was combing through the fan blogs for the show, and I came across these hate speeches directed at Sandy. They aren't the only negative comments out there, but this group of comments stood out because they are very threatening." The officer pointed at the screen. "This comment even mentions that she deserved to have the life squeezed out of her."

"Which, could be code for strangling." Oliver sighed. "I know that sometimes fans get very obsessed over a show, and will do anything or at least threaten to do anything to make sure it doesn't get ruined."

"I'm getting close to figuring out who posted the comments." The officer looked up at Oliver. "What's even more interesting is that it looks like the posts were made from right here in Little Leaf Creek."

"Wow!" Oliver raised his voice. "So, whoever posted these threats, was close enough to Sandy to follow through on them."

"Yes." The officer nodded.

"Do you think it could have been a local? Or someone that was here for the show?"

The officer stepped to the side as Oliver started scrolling through his computer.

"The posts go back months. I think they're from someone local." The officer tapped on the keyboard.

"Good work, keep looking into it and keep me updated." Oliver walked toward his office.

Cassie waited until he was in his office, then made her way to the front of the station. Her mind running through what she had learned.

CHAPTER 14

Tessa pulled up in her jeep, just as Cassie stepped out of the police station.

"Get in, we've been invited to lunch with Nel. She said our presence distracted Anton from attacking her." She raised an eyebrow.

"She saw us before Anton did." Cassie settled in the passenger seat.

"I know, but she may not know that. Did you find out anything new about Anton?" Tessa drove down the road toward the main strip in town.

"Not really. But I had some time to think about Nel. I don't know exactly what it is, but I just don't trust her." Cassie shook her head. "And I overheard something very interesting." She told Tessa about the threatening posts.

"So, it is possible that the posts will lead somewhere. But even if they lead somewhere, it doesn't mean the person is the murderer."

"It's definitely a good start, though." Cassie looked through the windshield.

"If it's a local, it could have been Kelvin. He seemed to genuinely hate her when he ranted about her in the diner, and he admitted that he didn't have an alibi."

"It's definitely a possibility." Cassie nodded. "Murder seems so extreme to me."

"It is. But it's still a possibility."

Cassie winced as Tessa pulled into the pizza place. She recalled her first and only date with Oliver which had been there. It hadn't gone well and they had decided to just remain friends. Is that where Sebastian and she were headed as well?

"Oh, this place."

"I know, they don't make the best pizzas. But we're not here for the food, we're here for the information. I agree with you about Nel. Something is off about her. Let's see what we can find out. I'll take the lead on this one." Tessa headed through the door of the restaurant, with Cassie right behind her.

"There you are!" Nel waved to the two of them. "Please sit." She turned off her tablet and slid it to the side. "I'm sorry, I've been fending off questions from all of the actors in the show. Everyone wants to know if recording the episode has been canceled, at least for the moment."

"Is it?" Tessa sat down across from her.

"I think we should go through with it." Nel shrugged. "It's the best way to honor Sandy's memory. She would be furious if any of us decided to cancel production over her death."

"I think she'd be a bit more furious that her murderer is still running free." Tessa looked into Nel's eyes. "You must be suspicious of the people you work with?"

"Why should I be?" Nel squared her shoulders as she looked back at Tessa. "For all I know it was some local nut who wanted to make a name for themselves, or maybe was obsessed with Sandy."

Cassie glanced away, hoping that her expression wouldn't give away how true that might be.

"That may be true, but there are plenty of suspects that were working with her every day. The people closest to her would be the best suspects. But you know that, don't you?" Tessa's stern expression gave way to a small smile.

"Yes, my research does point to that. Which is exactly why the location of the murder, and the recent upheaval between Sandy and Anton, would make him the prime suspect." Nel looked over at Cassie. "Is he still in custody, do you know?"

"I'm not sure." Cassie shifted in her chair. She guessed that Anton would be held for at least a few hours, but she doubted that Oliver would keep him too long, unless he found actual proof he was involved in the murder.

"So, you do suspect him?" Tessa pressed.

"I never said that." Nel looked back at her. "But I'm sure the police do. Or am I wrong about that?"

"I'm not sure, but I imagine he must be a suspect. Which is why I'm trying to find out what you think." Tessa raised an eyebrow. "Let's not play games anymore. You asked us to come here. Do you really think that Anton is the murderer?"

"I don't have to answer your questions, Tessa. In case you've forgotten, you don't carry a badge anymore." Nel looked over at Cassie. "And you never have. That's right, I've done my research on you, too, ever since you started poking around. Maybe, you have too much free time on your hands if you can spend so much of it playing amateur detectives."

"You can go on about badges and hand out your insults all you want, but you still haven't answered me. Which leads me to believe that you'd rather not give an honest answer." Tessa shrugged. "You may not want to say that he could be guilty, but you do believe that he might be. Otherwise, you wouldn't have called the police today. The difference between talking to me, and talking to someone with a badge, is I can't make you testify under oath in a trial, and they can. So, if there is something you want to get off your chest, something that you're too scared to tell the police, because you don't want to hurt your friend's feelings, or your career, then now is the time to say it. What you say to me, will only help find the murderer, but it will never be part of an official record."

Cassie's heart skipped a beat as she watched Tessa work. There were times when it became almost impossible to recognize the woman she now considered a friend, instead she transformed into a person Cassie had never had the chance to meet, a woman who had once very proudly worn a badge.

"It's probably nothing." Nel paused as the waitress delivered a large pizza, then looked back at Tessa. "That's why I haven't said anything. It seems like such a silly thing to mention."

"As observant as you are, I doubt that it is silly." Tessa smiled. "Out with it, Nel, this isn't a television show, this is real life. There won't be any tidy ending that wraps it all up, unless everything is out in the open."

"It's just, Anton's so passionate about his work. He's very dedicated to this show. He was pretty upset when Sandy hated his parents' property. But it got worse when he overheard someone say that Sandy was meeting with some other writer. I think he was worried about being replaced. He can get intense about the scenes, and the dialogue, but most of the time he's harmless. I just don't know if that was the case this time. Especially, after what I saw in the house."

"What did you see?" The words popped out of Cassie's mouth before she could stop them.

"There's a secret room. I guess, it's not really secret, but kind of hidden. I found him in it this morning when I got to the house. He'd left the pocket door open. It blends with the wall, if you didn't know it was there, you would never see it. I saw him cleaning up two broken glasses, and an overturned table. I ran back outside and knocked on the door like I'd never seen him." Nel sighed. "I know the two of them met late last night. But that's all I know. Okay?"

"Okay." Tessa nodded. "That's quite a bit of

information actually. Do you know if anyone saw or heard from Sandy after their meeting?"

"I have no idea. Sandy was notorious for doing her own thing. I didn't ever bother keeping track of her. The only reason I knew about the meeting is because Anton was so nervous about it. He asked me for some tips on how to keep Sandy calm while they talked. I had no idea what to tell him, she's unpredictable." Nel picked up a slice of pizza. "Eat up before it gets cold. I'm sure it's amazing."

Despite the look of the droopy, greasy pizza, Cassie dug in. Her stomach rumbled with the need for food, and her mind rumbled with the need for answers.

As Tessa continued to chat with Nel, Cassie watched the woman across from her. For someone who had called the police because she believed she was alone with a killer, she appeared fairly calm. Even when she confessed to having arguments with Sandy, her demeanor didn't change. Was she just a laid back person, or was she trying to cover up how she really felt?

"Now that Sandy is gone, who takes her position?" Tessa pushed her plate back, then finished off her water.

"I guess, I will. I mean, it just makes sense, I know so much about the show." Nel shrugged.

"I guess it's not such a bad thing for you that she's gone then." Tessa stood up from her chair.

"Don't be ridiculous. It's a terrible thing. It's a tragedy!" Nel frowned.

"Of course it is." Tessa nodded. "Thanks for lunch."

Cassie stood up as well.

"Don't get the wrong idea in your head, Tessa." Nel narrowed her eyes. "I had nothing to do with Sandy's death."

"I didn't say you did." Tessa stared at her for another long moment, then turned and walked away.

CHAPTER 15

"A bit defensive, wasn't she?" Tessa closed the door to her jeep.

"Very." Cassie shook her head. "But I'm not so sure about her motive. Could she really be certain that she would take over as producer? The studio could easily replace her with someone else."

"Maybe she was prepared to risk it. But that may not have been her only motive, but it could have been a nice bonus." Tessa turned into the driveway. "I'll call and update Ollie about the hidden room." She got out of the jeep and looked up at the house.

Harry ran up to the gate and barked as he spun around a few times.

"We saw each other about an hour ago, Harry."

Cassie smiled. "Did you miss me?" She laughed as she walked over to the gate.

Tessa walked up behind her and opened the gate.

"You might as well say hello to him."

Cassie walked through the gate and bent down to greet him.

"Hi pup." She rubbed behind his ears.

As Cassie stood up she heard a loud bleat. Two goats came running toward them.

"Uh oh." Tessa laughed. "I think they're hungry for treats." They ran straight toward Cassie and Tessa. Before they could reach them, Harry turned around and ran behind the goats. The goats changed direction with Harry hot on their tails.

"Saved by the dog!" Cassie laughed.

"I better get them fed. Before they jump the fence and help themselves. They're a bit spoilt. You would think a garden full of foliage would be enough to keep them full, but apparently not, they love their treats." Tessa smiled at Cassie. "We'd both better get some rest before tomorrow. I promised to be there by eight in the morning with the boys and the cookies."

"I'll be here to help." Cassie pointed to the back. "Speaking of the boys. They are so fast. Looks like they're coming back around again." She laughed as the two goats ran from the back with Harry still behind them.

"Okay, okay." Tessa laughed. "I better feed them."

Cassie watched Harry, Gerry and Billy who turned and followed after Tessa, then she walked through the gate that led to her own house. She stepped inside, and flipped the light on.

As Cassie walked through to the kitchen, she recalled the mess she'd left behind. She had been distracted by the murder and hadn't cleaned it up yet. She turned on the kitchen light, anticipating the pile of tiles and tools scattered all over the counter. Instead, she saw a backsplash behind her sink. Each tile was perfectly lined up. The tools were in the toolbox. She wiped her fingertips across the counter and realized it had been cleaned.

"Sebastian?" Cassie continued to stare at the tiles. Why would he let himself into her house with the key she gave him, and finish tiling her backsplash without so much as a word to her? She pulled out her phone to make sure she hadn't missed any messages or calls. Still, there hadn't been a single word.

Stunned, Cassie wondered for a moment what she should do. She guessed the only polite thing to do was to say thank you. She leaned back against the counter and dialed Sebastian's number. As she listened to the rings, she promised herself she wouldn't be weird. She'd just be grateful. Clearly, he had made an effort to show that he cared. When his voicemail picked up, her muscles tensed. No answer? He had to know that she would call to say thank you. So, why wouldn't he answer? He was probably busy. She was just being paranoid.

The beep sounded. She froze.

What could she say?

Not finding the right words, Cassie ended the call.

"Great, now there's a message from me, with nothing on it. No thank you, no why aren't you answering the phone, just nothing." Cassie sighed as she pressed the phone against her forehead. She couldn't call back, or he might think she was stalking him. Instead, she typed out a quick text.

Thanks for all your hard work.

Cassie hit send before she could second guess herself. As she stared at the words on the screen, she realized they were just as awkward as the empty message she'd left.

Cassie turned her phone off, and promised herself a good night's sleep.

The next morning, she found not a single

message in return. Maybe he'd worn himself out and gone to sleep early? But she'd never known Sebastian to sleep past five-thirty. It was already after seven.

"Oh, the Christmas Fair!" Cassie bolted out of bed and hurried to get ready. As she did, thoughts of the conversations from the day before flowed through her mind. She wondered if Anton had been released yet, or if Oliver had managed to get him to confess anything.

As Cassie crossed between her house and Tessa's, she spotted two goats in the back of her jeep.

"Looking beautiful, boys." Cassie grinned as she noticed the bandanas tied around their necks.

"You would not believe how long it took me to get those to stay tied. The boys kept moving around, they don't like being spruced up." Tessa rolled her eyes as she stepped out of the house. "Can you grab the cookies? I don't think they'll survive the drive with these two monsters."

"Sure thing." Cassie gave Harry a light pat as she walked past him into the house.

He whimpered.

"I'm sorry, Harry, but you can't come this time." Tessa scratched under his chin. "Today the goats get to go with me."

"Aw, poor guy. Are you sure we can't bring him?" Cassie stacked up three containers of cookies and carried them to the front door.

"No way. He'll get too excited. I need to keep track of the goats, and he'll want to be in charge of everything." Tessa shook her head.

"I can take him in my car." Cassie patted Harry's head.

Tessa looked from Cassie's pleading eyes into Harry's.

"Okay, you convinced me."

"Great." Cassie smiled as she grabbed his leash.

Harry spun around in a circle and then followed after Cassie.

"I'm getting soft in my old age." Tessa swung the door closed, then headed down the steps toward the jeep. Cassie noticed her limp. She knew that Tessa had been shot while trying to protect Oliver when they were working a case together. The limp always reminded Cassie that Tessa had a colorful past, and that she was a strong and determined woman. "I can't believe I let you talk me into this."

"Tessa, it's going to be great. What better opportunity to scope out our suspects?" Cassie smiled.

"Which of our suspects do you think is going to

show up at the Christmas Fair?" Tessa raised an eyebrow. "I don't think Hollywood types are too interested in goats or local bake sales."

"You never know." Cassie shrugged. "They're stuck here, what else are they going to do with their time? I'll meet you there." She carried the cookies with Harry close behind back to her driveway. She set the cookies carefully in the passenger seat and Harry on the back seat.

The Christmas Fair lasted three days, and although it was a small town, Cassie guessed that it would generate interest from other nearby towns as well. When she had originally planned on attending, it never crossed her mind that she might also be trying to help solve a murder instead of just helping to sell homemade Christmas decorations.

Located in the sprawling park on the outskirts of town, the Christmas Fair featured several booths from businesses in the area, as well as independent crafters. Many of the booths were still being erected, and the crowd was thin as she parked near the entrance. She crossed through the archway entrance laden with colorful garland and Christmas lights that would be illuminated in the evening. It took only a second for her to spot Tessa and the goats in the petting zoo area.

"Cassie, let me take those over to the stand." Tessa took the containers of cookies from her. "I think I spotted Kelvin over there."

"Really?" Cassie's eyes widened. "That's surprising."

"I thought so, too, I want to see what he's up to. I'll take Harry with." Tessa grabbed Harry's leash. "Will you keep an eye on the boys? I'm not sure this scrawny fence is going to keep them in." She gave the wire fence a light smack.

"Sure, I'll stay with them." Cassie watched as Tessa walked with Harry alongside sniffing the ground toward Kelvin. She guessed that the fair had lots of new and interesting smells for Harry to investigate.

Gerry nuzzled her hand through the fence.

"Sorry buddy, I don't have any snacks with me." Cassie turned around to pet the top of his head. As she did, she bumped into the fence, which bowed inward from her weight. The latch on the makeshift gate, unhooked, and Gerry headed straight for the opening it created.

"No! No Gerry!" Cassie gasped as she tried to get to the latch before Gerry could escape.

The goat squeezed through the gate before she

could get it to close completely again, and ran as fast as he could.

"Gerry! Get back here!" Cassie gasped as the goat bolted past a clown on stilts.

The clown wavered, but managed to regain his balance.

Cassie chased after the goat as he continued to run through the crowd in the direction of the parking lot. Her heart raced as she worried that he might get hit by a car. She managed to grab his collar just as he reached the edge of the parking lot.

"Oh, you silly goat, you have no idea how much danger you were in." She sighed as she hugged the goat.

Still trying to catch her breath, Cassie looked up at the sound of a familiar voice.

"I've told you enough times, Stephanie, when are you going to start listening to me?" Sebastian stepped in front of a blonde woman who tried to move past him. Cassie recognized her from seeing her with Sebastian outside the diner.

"When are you going to let me live my life?" Stephanie moaned, then shook her head. "You are obsessed, you know that? You need to back off!"

"Don't tell me to back off!" Sebastian glared at

her. "I love you, Stephanie, I'm not going to let you do this!"

Cassie's heart dropped as she stared at the pair, who were so caught up in their conversation and far enough away, not to notice her. Sure, her relationship with Sebastian was new, she didn't expect him to declare his love for her, but clearly he had no problem declaring his love for Stephanie. She caught the tip of her tongue between her teeth and bit down in an attempt to hold back her emotions. Overhearing the conversation was embarrassing enough, but if he caught her crouched there with her arms around a goat, while he argued with the woman he really loved, she would be mortified.

"Let's go, Gerry." Cassie pleaded with the goat as she tugged him back toward the crowd. If she could just get away from the parking lot, she was sure that Sebastian would never know she was there.

Gerry had other ideas. He jerked forward in an attempt to get away from her.

"Stop!" Cassie tugged Gerry harder, then winced as the goat bleated in protest.

"Cassie?" Sebastian locked eyes with her as she looked up at him.

CHAPTER 16

The shock of Sebastian looking straight at her distracted Cassie from the goal of keeping the goat in her arms. Gerry saw his chance and broke free.

"Gerry!" Cassie gasped as the goat ran even faster. She chased him through a crowd of people just entering the fair, but lost sight of him when he ran around a large Christmas tree. She jogged around the tree and stopped short at the sight of Sebastian holding onto Gerry's collar.

"Lose someone?" Sebastian's hand ruffled through Gerry's fur as he met Cassie's eyes.

Cassie's throat tightened before she could form a word. She had been thinking about what she would say the next time she saw Sebastian, but she hadn't expected to see him right then. She cleared her throat, then nodded.

"Gerry, I lost Gerry."

"I gathered that." Sebastian grinned as he released the goat to her. "It was fun watching you chase Gerry, though."

"Fun?" Cassie held tight to Gerry's collar.

"Sure." Sebastian frowned as he studied her. "What's wrong, Cassie? You don't seem like yourself."

"I'm fine." Cassie took a breath and a step back from him. "Just busy with the Christmas Fair. I should get back."

"Cassie, wait." Sebastian reached for her hand. "I know, I never got to tell you what happened the other night."

"Don't worry about it." Cassie cast a brief smile over her shoulder. "You don't have to tell me anything. We were just having fun, right?"

"What? Cassie?" Sebastian's eyes narrowed. "I think we need to talk."

"Nope." Cassie waved her hand as she urged the goat to take a few steps forward. "No need at all to talk. I get the picture, trust me."

"Cassie." Sebastian lowered his voice as he stepped toward her. "I don't think you do."

"Thanks, by the way." Cassie frowned as Gerry tried to tug out of her grasp. "For finishing the backsplash. But I could have done it, I was going to do it."

"I'm sorry, I knew it was on your list of things to get done and I needed a distraction. I still need to finish it off." Sebastian pulled off his baseball cap and ran his hand back through his hair as he sighed. "I guess I should have asked you first."

"That might have been best." Frustration rippled through her as she recalled the way he'd spoken to Stephanie. How could he just stand there, as if none of that had happened? "In fact, I can handle the rest of the repairs just fine on my own. I'd like to give my spare key to Tessa, since she's a closer neighbor, in case anything ever happens." She stumbled over her words as she watched his expression shift from confusion to something she couldn't quite define.

"Cassie, what's happened? I know it must have been horrible to find Sandy like that, and I haven't been there for you like I should have been, I'm sorry about that. If you just give me a chance to explain." Sebastian caught her fingertips just before she pulled her hand away.

"There's nothing to explain. Just leave it in the mailbox."

Desperate to escape Sebastian's determined gaze, Cassie grabbed the goat's collar, and hurried back toward the crowd. She couldn't talk to Sebastian about what she'd seen. It was too hurtful. She knew their relationship was over, but she didn't want to have the conversation, not until she was calm, and could handle the way he casually walked away from her. It was silly for her to have even entertained the idea of romance, but Sebastian had pulled her in with his charm and his warmth. She wanted to focus on helping solve the murder not worrying about their relationship.

"Cassie, are you alright?" Tessa walked up to her with a hot cup of coffee as she settled Gerry back inside the pen. Cassie was relieved to see that Billy was still inside it.

"I am now. Gerry escaped but I managed to track him down." Cassie couldn't bring herself to look at Tessa as she took the cup of coffee. "Thanks for this. What did Kelvin have to say?"

"He claims he intends to show his face everywhere to make sure that Oliver got the message that he's not the least bit afraid of him, or the rumors flying around town." Tessa took a sip of her coffee. "He's also running a booth for his friend here later."

"Do you think he would be here like this drawing attention to himself, if he was the killer?" Cassie looked in his direction. She watched as he shook a few hands, then broke into loud laughter.

"If he's devious enough, yes. It does make him look innocent to most. It's also the best way to deal with a false rumor. He'd look far more guilty if he was hiding out, don't you think?" Tessa walked over to the fence and tested it. "This is going to have to get strengthened or the boys are going to get out again."

Cassie opened her mouth to explain that Gerry had gone for quite an adventure, but she decided against it. She didn't want to talk about her encounter with Sebastian, not yet. As Tessa walked off to insist on the fence being strengthened, Cassie looked back toward the last place she had seen Sebastian. Whoever Stephanie was, she knew that she was a lucky woman. Cassie realized that her life in Little Leaf Creek had changed. As much as she would miss Sebastian being part of it, it had still become her home. She didn't feel any desire to leave it. Instead, the spark of determination to help keep it safe fired up within her again.

As Tessa walked back over to her, Cassie met her eyes.

"Let's go have another look at Anton's property. We need to figure out exactly where Sandy was killed. I think that will tell us more about who might have done it."

"That's a good idea, though I'm not sure what we'll find that Ollie might have missed. It doesn't hurt to have another look." Tessa waved to the woman overseeing the petting zoo, then led the way toward the parking lot with Harry by her side. It looked like Harry was ready for a new adventure. "Do you want to drop your car off at home. And we can travel together?"

"Sure."

After Cassie dropped her car at home, she got into Tessa's jeep which was waiting on the road for her.

"Was that Sebastian I saw at the fair earlier?" Tessa watched as Cassie buckled her seatbelt.

"I don't know." Cassie shrugged.

"Cassie." Tessa glanced over at her. "Let's not start keeping the truth from each other. I'm perfectly okay with you telling me to mind my own business, but I prefer honesty. Okay?"

"Okay." Cassie nodded. "Mind your own business, Tessa." She paused, then added in a whisper. "Please."

"Understood." Tessa started the jeep. "But if you want to talk about it, I can probably give you some terrible advice."

"I'm sure you can." Cassie laughed. "Let's get over there. It's time this killer was caught, so everyone can go back to enjoying the Holiday."

As they drove toward the property, Cassie focused her thoughts on the matter at hand. If Kelvin had been at the property, what had brought him there? Had he gone to confront Sandy? Had he gone with the intention of killing her? How had he even known she would be there?

"We know that Sandy saw Anton, Craig, and Heather, the night before she was killed. But what about Kelvin? If he killed her, wouldn't there be something that placed him at the crime scene? I'm sure that Ollie is going over all of Sandy's phone records, but Kelvin might not have gone that route. I get the feeling that he wouldn't have warned her about his visit. Which means that somehow he knew Sandy was there." Cassie glanced over at Tessa. "Do you think it was Heather?"

"It's possible." Tessa nodded. "They're both locals, they might be in close contact. Let's see what we can find." She turned down the road that led to the property.

Once they arrived at Anton's property, Cassie led Tessa and Harry across the driveway, to the shed which still had police tape around it.

"This is where we found her." Cassie stood in front of the shed door near a collection of overgrown grass and bushes. She shivered at the memory of the moment she and Mirabel had discovered Sandy.

"I see." Tessa looked around. "Do you remember anything at all from this moment? Anything that caught your eye? Anything that seemed off?"

"Anything other than the dead body?" Cassie glanced over at her.

"Yes, anything other than that." Tessa's tone was as firm as her gaze.

"No. Nothing." Cassie sighed. "I'm sorry. I've been through this with the police. I didn't hear anything, or notice anything strange."

"If Oliver's theory is right, Sandy wasn't killed here. If we could find the place where she was killed, it could change everything." Tessa looked toward the house. "Ollie found the hidden room, and collected what evidence was inside. He said he found a few shards of glass, but as Nel claimed, Anton had cleaned up most of it." She shook her head. "That doesn't help Anton's case any."

"No, I'm sure it doesn't." Cassie walked toward the house. "There were no drag marks there?" She looked over at Tessa. "If we're assuming that Sandy's body was moved, then I would think there would be some kind of drag marks."

"Unless the person was strong enough to carry her." Tessa paused as she looked back toward the shed. "If we assume that Sandy was murdered somewhere inside of the house, which we don't know for sure, but if we assume that, then it would be a good amount of distance to move a body. If she was carried, the person would have had to be pretty strong."

"Like Craig." Cassie raised an eyebrow. "Kelvin and Heather don't seem strong enough to me."

"Yes, like Craig. Or maybe Anton. Nel is pretty thin, but she did look muscular to me." Tessa narrowed her eyes, then nodded. "Of course, it could have been Kelvin and Heather. Right?"

"Oh, I hadn't thought of that!" Cassie paused beside the front porch of the house. "It could have easily been the two of them, and if we believe that Heather is the one that tipped Kelvin off to Sandy being here, then maybe they worked together to get rid of her, too."

"The house has been taped off again. Let's look through the windows and see if we can find anything. We need to look for anything that might stand out, anything that would indicate the body was moved. A missing tablecloth, some furniture moved aside. I really think she was killed somewhere in this house. We have to find out where." Tessa and Harry started up the porch steps.

Cassie followed after them, but paused at the sight of movement through the front window.

"Tessa, we're not alone!"

Harry lunged toward the front door in the same moment it swung open.

"Tessa." Oliver pushed the door open wider and

stepped out onto the porch. "And, Cassie. Why am I not surprised to see the two of you here?" He bent down to give Harry a pet. "Hi buddy." From the speed of Harry's wagging tail and the wide smile on Oliver's face, they were obviously happy to see each other.

"We're just taking a quick look." Cassie detected the instant tension between Tessa and Oliver, though it didn't feel as thick as it used to. "We're not causing any harm."

"How could you?" Oliver sighed as he glanced back at the house. "This place has already been trampled through by who knows how many people. I doubt that I'll be able to come up with any untainted evidence, now, and the techs will be here shortly to finish processing the scene. The property is huge."

"You haven't figured out where the murder actually took place, have you?" Tessa settled her eyes on Oliver.

"Yes, I think I have. I think it was in the living room. We can tell from the flooring and what Anton's mother said, that a rug is missing. Unfortunately, we haven't been able to find it, yet. The officers and techs are on their way out here to complete their search."

"Has Anton been released?" Cassie asked.

"Not yet, I'm going to release him today, I just don't have enough to hold him." Oliver shook his head. "Even with the broken glass I found, it's not enough to prove that he actually killed Sandy. He claims he found the broken glass in the room and cleaned it up for his parents." He turned to look at them both. "And honestly I'm not convinced that he did it. If he wanted to, he would have had plenty of opportunity to do it. We know that he was here alone with Sandy. If he wanted to kill her, why would he move her body to where he did? He grew up on this property, there's many places that he could have moved her body. Why to the shed where he knew it would probably be found quickly?"

"Maybe he didn't have enough time?" Tessa shook her head. "Maybe he thought he would be caught in the act."

"According to her time of death, he had time. The medical examiner's best estimate is a window between about midnight and three in the morning. Mirabel and Cassie found her body just before six in the morning. That gave him at least three hours between the time he killed her, and the time anyone else showed up." Oliver nodded.

"Three hours before I showed up, with Mirabel.

But maybe someone else was nearby. It's a huge house. Maybe someone was hiding out inside. Or maybe someone else came out to see Sandy."

"Maybe, but it's pretty odd to go out to visit someone so late, and if someone had been hiding, how would Anton know?" Oliver shook his head. "I just don't think he would have put her body there."

"We also noticed there weren't any drag marks." Tessa turned to face Oliver. "It seems to us that the body must have been carried. Did you find any shoeprints in the area?"

"No. The ground has been so dry that shoeprints likely didn't make much of a mark. But you're right, there should have been drag marks. I agree, that she was likely carried. Which makes our suspect a strong one, and probably male." Oliver held up one hand as Cassie opened her mouth. "I know women are capable of carrying a body. But Sandy wasn't a small woman. She was quite tall. Nel seems pretty strong, but she's not very tall. It would have been hard for her to carry a taller person. I imagine Kelvin could move the body easily."

"We had considered that maybe Kelvin and Heather were working together." Cassie looked at him. "Heather might have been the one to tip Kelvin off to Sandy's presence, and maybe the two of them decided to get rid of her."

"That's an interesting theory." Oliver nodded. "We've been trying to pin down what exactly was used to strangle Sandy. So far we've been able to eliminate rope. The marks left behind were flat, and not abrasive."

"Like a belt?" Tessa glanced at him.

"Yes, possibly. But it was quite thin." At the sound of an engine, Oliver looked toward the driveway. "The techs are here. I'll catch up with you later." He gave Harry a pat and another treat.

"No wonder he likes you." Tessa laughed. "You keep giving him treats."

CHAPTER 18

Cassie, Tessa and Harry walked down the stairs of Anton's house.

"Let's have a look around outside." Tessa steered Cassie around the side of the building. "If the rug is missing, where did it go?" She raised an eyebrow. "Even if the killer used it to wrap up Sandy's body, it wasn't around here when the body was found."

"Which means it was likely disposed of, you're right."

Tessa glanced in the trashcans at the back of the house.

"These are empty. The police likely took all of the contents to look through."

Harry began sniffing the ground more intensely

and dragging Tessa behind him. She was jolted forward.

"What can you smell, buddy?" Tessa laughed as she followed behind Harry. "Food?"

"I don't think the killer would have thrown the rug out in the trashcans. It's too easy to find. Sandy was moved, I'm betting any evidence left behind was hidden." Cassie followed Harry and Tessa around the side of the house, then winced. "Ugh, what is that smell?"

"A compost pile, city girl." Tessa chuckled, then looked over the small pit. "A very neglected one, and it shouldn't smell this bad. If it hadn't been touched in a while, the smell would have faded." Harry tugged at the leash in an effort to get to the compost. Tessa shortened the leash and held tightly to it. "Oh, no you don't. There is no way you are digging through that."

"Look, the stuff on top is pretty damp. With how dry it's been, it shouldn't be." Cassie pointed to the mixture of soil and compost on the top of the pile.

"You're right, someone's been digging in here." Tessa handed Cassie Harry's leash and took out some gloves from her pocket. "You can never be too prepared." She began to roll up her sleeves.

"Oh, Tessa, no!" Cassie gasped as she watched the woman crouch down in front of the pile.

"To solve a crime, sometimes you have to get a little dirty, Cassie." Tessa rolled her eyes, then sank her hands into the pile.

Harry barked eagerly and pulled in Tessa's direction, but Cassie held tightly to the leash. There was no way she wanted Harry to get into the compost.

"Oh gross!" Cassie gasped as she looked away from the sight of the bugs that scattered away from Tessa's hands. She held Harry's leash tighter.

"You alright there, Cassie?" Oliver grinned as he walked up to her.

"Please make her stop, Ollie!" Cassie winced and refused to look back at Tessa.

"Here it is! Here's the rug." Tessa pulled up what looked like the corner of a rug and smiled as she looked at Oliver and Cassie. "I'll let you handle it from here, Ollie."

"Great." Oliver took a deep breath, then rolled up his sleeves and put on some gloves. "Hopefully, we can salvage something from it. The techs were going to process this today."

"I'm going to use the hose to clean up." Tessa

walked toward the hose attached to the back of the house.

"Tessa, you'll freeze." Cassie pulled off her coat. "You can use this to dry off."

"I'll be alright, Cassie, it's not too cold out here."

"Stop, Tessa!" Oliver stood up. "That hasn't been processed, yet."

"Look at this." Tessa gasped as she looked at the hose.

"What is it? What did you see?" Cassie peered past her at the area around the hose.

"Compost! Someone else washed off over here. See? The ground is wet. Stay back, there might be some evidence to be found here. Ollie!" Tessa waved him over and pointed out the compost on the tap. "I bet whoever buried the rug in the compost pile, washed off over here."

"I think I see a bit of blood as well." Oliver crouched down and peered closely at the metal surface. "We have a lot of ground to cover today."

"I still need to get cleaned off." Tessa looked back toward the house.

"There's a tap on the other side of the house that's already been processed." Oliver nodded to her as he began snapping pictures of the potential evidence.

Cassie dragged Harry away from the compost pile and followed after Tessa.

"I'm so glad we came out here today." Tessa walked over to the hose on the other side of the house and turned on the faucet. "We've made some good discoveries."

Cassie looked back toward the hose.

"It's odd that there's blood, isn't it? If someone is strangled, there's not usually much blood involved, is there?"

"Not usually, no." Tessa dried her hands off on her shirt, and headed for the jeep. "I think we'd better head back. I promised Doris at the bake sale table, that I would bring her another dozen cookies this afternoon. We'd better get on that. Maybe Ollie will uncover something that will solve the case, until then we just have a lot of guesses, and not a lot of evidence."

"Wait, Craig had cuts on his hand, remember?" Cassie caught up to her at the jeep. "Maybe he washed his hands off with the hose."

After putting Harry in the backseat Cassie got in the front.

"Maybe, but why wouldn't he go inside to do it? He claimed he was helping Sandy work out how to use the property as a setting. Sandy had access to the house. Why wouldn't he go inside? It would be easier to clean it in the house. So, what if he didn't cut his hand the way he claims?" Tessa started the jeep. "Maybe, he somehow cut his hand while he was killing Sandy."

"Maybe. Maybe Oliver will find more blood." Cassie shook her head. "Romance can be terribly dangerous."

"Not true romance, Cassie, between two people that care about each other." Tessa sighed as she met her eyes. "You should really consider giving Sebastian another chance. At least talk to him about it."

"Me?" Cassie frowned as she looked out through the window. "Trust me, Tessa, he doesn't want another chance. He's already moved on."

"I know Sebastian. He's loyal to a fault. His parents divorced when he was young and he moved to Little Leaf Creek to live with his grandparents. He visited his parents, they never came to see him here, at least I've never seen them. I don't know too much about it, but I think that seeing his family torn apart has made him who he is. And he is the most loyal person I have ever met." Tessa glanced over at her.

"I didn't know that." Cassie glanced back at Tessa. "But I still think he has moved on."

"I've seen the way he looks at you, Cassie, he didn't just move on from that." Tessa pulled into her driveway and parked the jeep, then she turned in her seat to stare straight at her. "You need to hear him out."

"Wait a minute." Cassie frowned as she looked back at her. "Did you talk to him?"

"No. I'm trying not to get into the middle of things. But the Sebastian that you're describing, isn't the Sebastian that I know." Tessa let Harry off his leash. He bounded up the front steps to the front porch. Tessa followed behind him.

"All that matters right now is finding Sandy's killer." Cassie followed her up the steps. "Let's focus on that."

CHAPTER 19

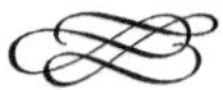

Despite her words to Tessa, Cassie's mind focused on Sebastian as she helped roll out the cookie dough. While Tessa cut out the cookies, Cassie's thoughts explored alternative explanations for Sebastian's behavior. He had declared his love for Stephanie, how else was she supposed to interpret that? Her gaze settled on Tessa as she began to place the cut cookies on a baking sheet. Tessa claimed that she liked living alone, that she had no interest in a relationship, but maybe that wasn't true. Maybe she wanted to see Cassie and Sebastian continue a relationship, because in some way, it filled an empty spot within her.

"You know, I didn't come here looking for romance, Tessa?"

"I know." Tessa looked up at her, her eyes widened. "You came here for a fresh start, right?"

"Yes, a fresh start." Cassie began rolling out the next ball of dough. "I was married, I had a long relationship, and now that's over, and I want to move on."

"Here, cut those cookies out while I look something up on the computer." Tessa passed the cookie cutter to her.

"Okay." Cassie glanced at her as she headed for the table. "But do you understand what I'm saying, Tessa?"

"I understand." Tessa nodded. "I remember hearing something a while ago, it's probably nothing but I want to look into it more." She smiled as Harry lay down by her feet. She stroked his head, then sat up and began typing. A few minutes later she looked up from the screen. "I think I might have found something." She sat back in her chair. "About our friend Kelvin."

"Oh?" Cassie set the last cookie into the container and snapped the lid on. "What did you find?"

"Apparently, Sandy filed a lawsuit against him for defamation of character. It was a few years back, and it never went to court, but I was able to dig up the paperwork." Tessa turned the computer around toward Cassie. "In her complaint she describes his chronic behavior of accusing people of things. Apparently, Sandy wasn't the only person that supposedly ruined Kelvin's life. He's accused a doctor, a business owner, and even an ex-girlfriend of harming him in some way."

"Wow, I wasn't expecting that." Cassie skimmed over the text on the screen. "So, if this is a habit of his, that might mean he's not telling the whole truth about his experience with Sandy."

"Yes, that's true, but it may also mean that Kelvin had even more motivation to cause Sandy harm. If she had threatened to pursue the lawsuit, he might have been scared he would lose what little he has left. It could have inspired him to go after Sandy even more." Tessa turned the computer back toward her. "The lawsuit is a few years old, but if Kelvin confronted Sandy while she was here, then she could have easily threatened to start legal proceedings up again."

"Absolutely." Cassie nodded. She imagined a confrontation between Kelvin and Sandy. "If he saw her again, he was likely furious. He probably couldn't resist going after her. When she saw him, she probably just wanted to get rid of him, she already had enough problems to deal with. I can see how things could have easily gotten out of control. But it does beg the question, why did Sandy not pursue the lawsuit in the first place? She went to all the trouble to start it up, why didn't she take him to court?"

"That's a good question. Unfortunately, I'm not sure how to find the answer to that. The only person that would be able to answer that question is gone now." Tessa frowned. "I've yet to find anyone in her life that I would consider a friend, someone she might have confided in."

"We at least know that she spent some time with Craig." Cassie winced as she sat down at the table across from her. "Though, I'm not sure how much more information we can hope to get out of him after how I left things with him."

"But we also know that apparently Craig was just a toy to her. I doubt she would have confided anything in him. She was on the outs with Nel, she was furious with Anton, and really I'm not sure that there was anyone in her life that wasn't scared of her or dependent in some way upon her for their livelihood." Tessa closed her computer and sighed.

"So, we've hit a wall." Cassie stared across the

table at her. "That just means we're missing something."

"It does, but what?" Tessa shook her head.

"Well, even if she wasn't close with anyone she worked with, she still worked with them each day. My guess is the people around her knew a lot more about her life than they realize. I say we talk to a few of them again and see if anything else comes up. Starting with Craig. We know that he was at the property, we know that he was in a relationship with Sandy, and we know that she had a tendency to be cruel." Cassie stood up from the table. Harry stood as well. "Let's see what we can find out."

"I do think we need to speak to Craig again, but first I want to talk to Kelvin. If our hunch is right, and he had some kind of confrontation with Sandy, then we need to find out what happened between them. Don't forget, we know that someone who lives in Little Leaf Creek has been spewing some terrible things all over the internet about Sandy. Right now, Kelvin is our best suspect when it comes to the desire for revenge, the physical ability to move Sandy's body, and his behavior before and after her death." Tessa pushed herself up out of the chair. "If he and Heather did somehow work together to get rid of Sandy, then we need to find their connection, so that we can prove it."

"Okay, back to the diner? He might be there." Cassie picked up the container of cookies. "Should we drop these off first?"

"Actually, Kelvin mentioned that he was going to be working the booth at the fair for his friend again. So, I think we can take care of the cookie delivery and a conversation with him at the same time. If he's not there, then we can try the diner again."

"Great." Cassie gave Harry a light pet, then looked up at Tessa. "Hopefully, he'll be interested in telling the truth, but somehow I doubt it."

"Me too." Tessa sighed. "Do you want to come with again, Harry?" He ran straight over to his leash. "I guess so." She laughed and led the way back to her jeep. As she started it up, she looked over at Cassie. "I understand by the way, I really do."

"Understand what?" Cassie raised an eyebrow.

"That you're scared." Tessa put the jeep in drive and pulled out of the driveway.

"Scared of the killer?" Cassie shrugged. "I can't say that it doesn't leave me a little unsettled, but I think Sandy was targeted. I don't think her killer will be after anyone else."

"Not scared of that, no. Scared of whatever might

be between you and Sebastian." Tessa turned down the road and headed in the direction of the fair.

"Tessa." Cassie sighed and closed her eyes. "It's not that. It's not that at all. Listen, I spent so many years of my life being with someone who didn't really want to be with me. We fell out of love almost as quickly as we got married. I just don't want to be in that position again. Okay?" She shook her head. "Sebastian is a good person, you're right about that. In fact, he's a great person. But that doesn't mean that he's the right person for me, or that I'm the right person for him. If he's happier with someone else, then that's what I want for him. So, no meddling. Understand?"

"I understand." Tessa glanced away as a small smile crossed her lips.

Cassie frowned. She had the distinct impression that Tessa did not understand at all.

"Actually, why don't we cover more territory?" She pointed to the intersection they approached. "I want to speak to Heather again. She lives somewhere around here. You can talk to Kelvin and deliver the cookies, and I'll see what I can find out from her. Just let me out up here."

"Cassie, don't be angry with me." Tessa frowned. "I'm not trying to upset you, I promise."

"I know you aren't. I just want to see if I can speak to Heather." Cassie met her eyes. "Please let me out. I'll catch up with you later."

Without another word Tessa pulled the jeep to the side of the road and stopped. She stared through the windshield, as Cassie climbed out of the jeep. Cassie reached into the back and patted Harry on the head.

"I'll catch up with you later, buddy." She closed the door and started down the street.

Cassie started to turn back to say something to Tessa, but Tessa had pulled away before the words were formed. She sighed as she stared after the jeep. She'd worked hard to get in Tessa's good graces, but when it came to her interfering in her relationship with Sebastian, she had to draw a line, didn't she?

CHAPTER 20

Cassie frowned as she started down the sidewalk in the direction of Heather's address. She hadn't actually been there, but had looked it up not long after their first conversation. She had almost reached the row of small cottages when she noticed a person carrying a suitcase and a few bags down the front steps of a porch. The load was so large that it hid the person who carried it. She stepped forward, ready to offer to help, but before she could the suitcase slipped out of the person's hand and sailed past the last few steps.

"Great, just great!" A muffled voice groaned.

"Heather?" Cassie took a step back as the suitcase slammed down a few inches from her.

"Yes?" Heather dropped the rest of the bags

beside the suitcase, then frowned at the sight of Cassie. "Oh, it's you."

"What's going on?" Cassie looked over the pile of boxes and bags already stacked near the curb.

"What's wrong? You've never seen an eviction before?" Heather rolled her eyes, then rummaged in her purse. As she dug deep into the pockets, the thin, leather strap that hung over her shoulder broke apart from one side of the purse. The contents of the purse spilled out onto the sidewalk.

Cassie crouched down to pick up a rolling tube of lip gloss.

"Oh no! I thought I fixed that! Will anything go right for me, ever?" Heather let out a loud groan as she dropped down to her knees and began collecting her wallet, mints, and a hairbrush.

"Heather, what do you mean you're being evicted?" Cassie handed her the lip gloss. "Don't you have anywhere to go?"

"Oh?" Heather forced a smile. "Of course I do, Cassie. There are so many places that want people to move in who have zero money to pay the rent and zero money to put down for a deposit. I just can't seem to choose one."

"Heather." Cassie frowned as she noticed the

tears in the woman's eyes. "I'm so sorry. I didn't know you were having so much trouble."

"Don't be sorry, it's my own fault." Heather finished collecting the last of the items and tossed them back into her broken purse. "I was stupid. I pinned all of my hopes on the idea that Sandy would read and love my episode, my writing and would want me to work on the show. I was sure that my luck was about to turn around. But that wasn't the case. Now, I have to face the consequences." She sniffled, then looked over at her pile of possessions. "I just always thought things would work out somehow. But the truth is, life is stacked against people like me."

"Things will get better, even if this moment is a rough one."

"Great, I'll keep that in mind while I'm sleeping in the park tonight." Heather sat down on her suitcase. "If, I don't get kicked out by the police."

"Listen Heather, why don't you let me get you a room at the inn. At least for tonight, so you'll have a place to put your things, and to figure out what you're going to do next. I'm sure there's someone who can help." Cassie offered her hand to Heather. "You just have to have faith that things are going to straighten out."

"Spoken like someone who has never been evicted before." Heather crossed her arms. "I don't need your help, Cassie. I can handle this on my own."

"Please Heather? It's just one night." Cassie's heart ached at the thought of leaving her in the middle of the street with nowhere to go. Although, she had spent most of her life very wealthy, she'd grown up in a fairly impoverished town, in a community where no one was left to sleep outside, even if they had nowhere else to go. "I know it's not easy to accept help, but what are your other options?"

"Why would you even want to help me?" Heather glared at her. "You must get something out of it."

"Heather, I just don't want to see you without a roof over your head. I know it's not a permanent solution, but we can figure things out from there." Cassie sighed as she pulled her phone out of her purse. "I'll get us a cab so that we can gather all of your things. If you want, I can keep them at my house until you find a new place."

"You're up to something, don't think I don't know that." Heather crossed her arms as her cheeks reddened. "But you're right, I have no other choice."

"Great, then I'll just find a cab service." Cassie

frowned as she scrolled through the options. She was searching for one that offered service in Little Leaf Creek.

A familiar engine rumbled up beside her. She glanced up from the phone to see Sebastian's blue pickup truck.

"Ladies." He peered through the open window at the two of them. "Is everything okay here?"

"Sure it is." Cassie stared at him. "Why wouldn't it be?"

"Cassie here, thinks she's going to get a cab to come out to Little Leaf Creek." Heather smiled. "I thought I'd watch her try for a little while."

"Oh, Cassie." Sebastian's lips quirked into a knowing smile. "We're too far off the beaten path for that kind of service."

"Fine, then I'll just walk back to my place and get my car." Cassie turned back to Heather. "It won't take long, I promise."

"What exactly is happening here?" Sebastian stepped out of his truck, and onto the sidewalk. "Are you moving, Heather?"

"Not exactly. But Cassie said she'd help me out." Heather shrugged. "I just don't want to leave all my stuff here on the sidewalk."

"Well, let's load it up." Sebastian grabbed a few of

the bags. "There's plenty of room in the back of the truck."

"It's okay really." Cassie frowned. "I can just go get my car."

"Then I'll give you a ride to your car." Sebastian's eyes settled on hers. "We really need to talk."

"On second thought, we'll take you up on your offer." Cassie grabbed the suitcase and hauled it into the back of the truck. "Heather, you sit up front. I'll keep an eye on the stuff back here to make sure nothing falls out."

"Cassie." Sebastian stepped in front of her.

Cassie stepped around him and climbed up into the truck. "Let's go, I want to make sure that she gets settled and I need to get back to the fair soon."

"Whatever you say." Sebastian's jaw clenched as he loaded the last of Heather's possessions. Then he held the door open for Heather to climb in.

As Cassie heard the engine roar to life, she sensed that Sebastian wasn't going to simply let things go. The conversation she'd been avoiding was bound to happen, whether she liked it or not.

CHAPTER 21

Once Cassie had dropped Heather's stuff off at her house and had her settled at the inn, she headed back to the fair to meet up with Tessa. She'd managed to dodge Sebastian one more time, but her heart sank with the knowledge that he was going to insist on talking about things. It was one thing to break things off, another to discuss it. She'd rather just let the whole mess become a memory.

"Tessa!" She waved to her as she walked toward the goat pen.

"Cassie, just in time to give the goats a little snack." Tessa smiled as she handed her some treats to pass on.

"Great." Cassie held her hand out over the top of the fence, and laughed as the goats instantly nuzzled her palm in search of their treats. She felt something rub against her leg and looked down to see Harry with something in his mouth. "Hi buddy." She rubbed his head. "Is that a Santa's hat?" She laughed as she looked at Tessa.

"It is." Tessa rolled her eyes. "Harry here decided to tackle a Santa that was on display and steal the hat."

"Oh no, Harry." Cassie patted his head.

"Anyway, John, who runs the stand, said Harry could keep the hat. It's been in his mouth ever since." Tessa shook her head. "I offered to pay for the damage, but John said not to worry about it, the entertainment of watching Harry's antics was payment enough."

"I'm sure it was a good show." Cassie smiled. "How did it go with Kelvin?"

"He admitted to me that he went out to the property to speak to Sandy. He said that he wanted to convince her to put the past behind them. But she was already busy talking to someone else when he arrived."

"Who?" Cassie narrowed her eyes.

"Your friend, the writer." Tessa raised her eyebrows. "Did you happen to run into her?"

"Yes actually." Cassie's heart skipped a beat. "Did

he say anything else about seeing Heather there with Sandy?"

"He said that Heather was furious. She even tried to attack Sandy." Tessa lifted one shoulder. "But that's Kelvin's story. I'm not sure if that's what happened or not. What did you get from talking with Heather?"

Cassie winced as she explained the details of finding Heather homeless, and Sebastian's help.

"So, you put her up in the inn?" Tessa smiled as she shook her head. "You have such a good heart, Cassie."

"Well, what else was I supposed to do?" Cassie sighed as she brushed her palm off. "I couldn't exactly leave her there. All of her things were on the curb, and then her purse strap broke, and I just couldn't walk away."

"Wait a minute, her purse strap broke?" Tessa narrowed her eyes. "Did she get it caught on something?"

"No, it just came apart while she was looking through it. She said something about thinking that she had fixed it. I guess it had broken before. I'm not surprised it came apart, it was quite thin. The poor woman can't even afford to buy a new purse." Cassie gave the goats a few pets. "Even though I lived in luxury for a long time, I remember what it was like to make do with what I had when I was young. I don't have unlimited resources, but I have enough to be able to help someone that needs it. It seemed like the right thing to do."

"Cassie, I think your heart was in the right place, but I'm not so sure you helped the right person." Tessa turned to look at the crowd of people heading into the fair.

"Do you really think she did it?" Cassie met her eyes.

"Think about it. We know now that Heather wasn't just an aspiring writer who wanted some recognition, she was one hundred percent relying on Sandy giving her a job. It was her last chance at keeping herself afloat." Tessa gave a quick wave to someone in the crowd, then looked back at Cassie. "Which means when she was rejected, it had to be one of the most painful experiences of her life."

"I can see that." Cassie shivered as an icy wind swirled around her. "Yes, but that doesn't mean that she killed her. What would she get from that?"

"Maybe she just wanted to even the score for once. She wanted to see someone else lose?" Tessa pursed her lips, then continued. "We know that

Sandy was strangled, by something fairly thin and flat."

"Oh no." Cassie gasped as she recalled the sight of the purse strap. "You think that Heather used her purse to strangle Sandy, and that's how the strap broke?"

"I think it's possible." Tessa shook her head. "We can't know for sure, but it's possible."

"This is terrible!" Cassie tightened her jacket around her. "I might have just paid for a room for a murderer? I might have just put her under the same roof as a bunch of innocent people?"

"It's actually a good thing, Cassie. If Heather is the murderer, you've given her reason to trust you. Which means we might be able to find out more from her, or even set a trap for her. You've gotten us closer to her, and that might be what we need to solve this case."

"I don't know." Cassie sighed. "I feel like my instincts are all over the place right now." She frowned as she looked into the goat pen. "Don't you think it's getting a bit too cold out here for them?"

"It wasn't supposed to be this cold. It's only late afternoon and it's already starting to get dark." Tessa glanced up at the darkening sky. The Christmas lights began to shine in the dim light. Music played through the speakers throughout the area. Despite the festivities, Cassie still had the murder in the back of her mind.

"If Heather did this, she didn't do it alone. There's no way." Cassie shook her head as she rubbed her hands together to warm them. "She's tiny compared to Sandy. She couldn't have strangled her."

"But someone else could have used her purse strap. Someone who saw her there."

"Someone like Kelvin." Cassie nodded. "The problem is, if they were working together, why would Kelvin be confessing that he saw Heather there and that she attacked Sandy? Do you think he's trying to frame her?"

"I think that's possible. Maybe Heather wasn't leaving her house because she was evicted, maybe she's trying to get away from Kelvin. If he's the one who actually killed Sandy, maybe she's considering turning against him. With you laying the groundwork, showing her that she can trust you, she might just turn to you to tell the truth. But we can't push her too hard right now." Tessa took a deep breath. "Right now we need to just enjoy the fair. We don't want to tip either of them off to the idea that we're on to them."

"Good point." Cassie shivered again. "Aren't you cold, Tessa?"

"I'm starting to be." Tessa scrunched up her nose. "I think some hot chocolate would help with that."

"I'll get us some." Cassie walked over to the refreshment table. Her mind churned with each step. She liked the Heather and Kelvin theory, they were locals, but how well did they know each other? Would bonding over their hatred of Sandy really be enough to motivate them to kill?

"Two hot chocolates please." Cassie smiled at the woman behind the table.

"Sure. Marshmallows? Whipped cream?"

"Absolutely." Cassie grinned.

"Coming right up." She sighed as she picked up two cups. "It's just not the same this year, is it?"

"Oh, I wasn't here last year." Cassie shrugged. "But it seems pretty great to me."

"It's just the feeling of it." She frowned as she filled the cups. "There's no buzz, no excitement. I think everyone has that murder on their mind."

"I can understand that." Cassie piled some cash into the donation box. "But hopefully it will be solved soon."

"I'll believe that about as much as I believe it's going to snow in Little Leaf Creek." She rolled her eyes as she handed over the cups. "It hasn't snowed here in forever, and I can tell you, what happened on Anton's property is going to stay on his property. Even if the people around here had seen something, they wouldn't tell anyone. There's a bit of a code in these small towns, you know?"

"Is there?" Cassie narrowed her eyes as she studied the woman. She was yet another person she felt as if she recognized but whose name she couldn't place. She had met so many people since moving to Little Leaf Creek, it was hard for her to keep track of them all.

"Sure. If it's not your business, you don't say a word about it." She laughed. "Of course that doesn't apply to gossip, only the most serious things."

"I would think everyone here would want the murder solved." Cassie frowned as the hot cups started burning the tender skin of her palms.

"Oh, they do, but they don't want to be the ones to lock up a friend, or a neighbor." She smiled as she looked around at the crowd. "Loyalty is a big thing around here." She looked back at Cassie. "But I guess you don't know much about that, being new in town. I heard you were at Anton's house when Ollie took him in and locked him up. Didn't think twice about it, did you? Didn't try to help him, did you?"

"I couldn't have done anything. It's not like I called the police." Cassie's eyes narrowed as she took a step back from the table. The chill in the air wasn't just coming from the rapidly cooling temperature. "Thanks for the hot chocolate." She turned to walk away.

"Cassie!" A deep voice called out.

"Cassie." Craig waved to Cassie as he walked toward her.

"Hi Craig." Cassie smiled.

"I wanted to speak to you." Craig rubbed his hands together. He looked agitated.

"You did?"

"I've seen you with that cop. You're friends with him right?" Craig met her eyes.

"I am friends with Oliver, yes." Cassie set the cups of hot chocolate down on a small table. "Why?"

"You can tell him, I had nothing to do with Sandy's murder." Craig sighed as he sat down in a folding chair.

"Are you okay?" Cassie took a step closer to him.

"No, everything is falling apart." Craig shook his

head. "Sandy's gone now. But she lied to me before she died. She lied to me about everything."

"What do you mean, Craig?" Cassie studied the pain etched into his expression. "Did she break things off with you?"

"Yes, okay, she did! But she wasn't serious about it. I knew that. She would always get tense when we're filming an episode. But in the end, she would always come back to me. This time though, she took things too far. She told me that she was going to fire me if I kept arguing with her about it. So, I waited until I thought she would be alone. I just wanted to talk to her, away from everyone else, and reason with her. I was waiting for her in the house. I thought once we were alone I'd be able to convince her to forget about her little tantrum. But then she showed up with him."

"Him?" Cassie held her breath as she hoped that he would continue.

"Anton!" Craig scowled.

"She met with Anton that night?" Cassie nodded. "To talk about the episode?"

"I had to hide. I wanted to hear what they were saying. So, I ducked into a closet. I didn't close the door all the way, so I could see what they were up to." Craig narrowed his eyes. "Anton poured them both a drink, then he took her through a hidden door into another room. She wasn't supposed to be drinking, but I saw her take a sip. He was trying to convince her to still use his property as the location for the episode and to still pay his parents." He rolled his eyes. "Pathetic. He was practically begging her."

"Craig, then what happened?" Cassie raised her voice slightly.

"Then what happened?" Craig blinked, then stared at her. "She kissed him, but he pulled away. Then I heard her tell him that if he wanted to save his job, he was going to have to do something for her."

"Do what?" Cassie tried to keep him talking.

"When she said he was going to lose his job, he threw his glass on the floor. She told him that if he wanted to keep his job, he had to write Lionel's character out of the script."

"She wanted Lionel fired?" Cassie frowned. "But isn't he one of the lead actors?"

"He is. And he knows it. He wanted more pay." Craig grimaced. "Never satisfied, huh? He makes as much as I do. The show has less funds, but they have cut costs in other areas, not our pay, and he wanted even more."

"But don't you only have a small role on the

show?" Cassie played back her conversations with Lionel in her mind. Had she missed something? The truth was, she hadn't even really considered him a suspect.

"It was going to get bigger." Craig cleared his throat. "Anyway, I left after that. I knew I wouldn't be able to convince her of anything."

"Did you go back in the morning?" Cassie leaned closer to him. "To try to smooth things over with her?"

"The morning she was found?" Craig stared at her. "Of course not."

"But did you at least think about it? Did you wonder what she was up to, out there, all alone?" Cassie searched his eyes for any reaction.

"I didn't even know she was out there." Craig cleared his throat. "I figured she was with Anton working and then she went back to the inn. I had no idea she didn't make it back there." His eyes widened. "I don't want to talk about this anymore." He ran his hand across his forehead. "I keep thinking, maybe if I had tried to speak to her, maybe if I had just gone back out there or if I had stayed there, if I had just confronted her, I might have stopped what happened."

"But you didn't." Cassie pressed him once more, and studied his expression.

"No, I didn't!" Craig bolted to his feet as outrage creased his features.

"Alright, Craig, take it easy." Cassie eased back a few steps as his furious gaze locked to hers.

"No, I won't. I won't hear another person accuse me of hurting the woman I loved." Craig touched his chest.

"That's not what I'm doing, Craig." Cassie shook her head. "I just thought maybe you stayed there, maybe you went back there, maybe you heard, or saw someone, something, that might give a clue as to what happened to Sandy."

"I didn't." Craig collapsed back down into his chair and squeezed his eyes shut. "I didn't stay there, I didn't go back there, alright? I should have, but I didn't."

"Alright." Cassie nodded. "But you should really tell the police what you saw."

"Maybe." Craig looked at his watch, then stood up. "I better get back to the inn. I'm meeting with Nel."

"Are you sure you'll be okay?" Cassie smiled.

"Yes, thanks Cassie." Craig nodded. "I just needed to speak to someone and you're really the only one I know here. I can't talk to the cast and crew about it. I'm not that close to them. I hoped you would talk to Oliver for me."

"I think you should tell him yourself. It will be much better if you did."

"Okay." Craig nodded, then headed in the direction of the car park.

Cassie stared at him for a moment longer, then picked up the cups and turned and walked away. Did he speak to her so she would tell Oliver and cover his tracks? Was he the murderer? She wanted to believe that he was telling the truth, but she knew that grief could completely transform a person. Did Sandy breaking up with him and seeing her kiss Anton turn him into a killer?

CHAPTER 23

As the fair went into full swing, Cassie tried to focus on the festivities, but she was distracted by her conversation with Craig. She shared the conversation with Tessa, who was a little preoccupied trying to keep the goats inside the pen.

"Interesting, do you think he's lying? Do you think he did it, Cassie?"

"Maybe, I don't know." Cassie shook her head. "But he doesn't exactly have a lot of motive to murder Sandy."

"He saw her kiss another man. I'd say that's pretty good motive." Tessa shook her head. "Not everyone can be so casual about romance, Cassie."

"Tessa, not now." Cassie frowned.

"I mean it, though. If he saw Anton and Sandy

kiss, then he could have easily been thrown into a jealous rage." Tessa frowned. "I did like the idea of Heather and Kelvin working together, but maybe we're just trying too hard here. Anton was the most obvious suspect, but Craig certainly is a close second. Jealousy, betrayal can certainly lead to murder. It wouldn't surprise me if that's exactly what happened here."

"I don't know, I just can't see him doing this. He was so cute as a kid. His father was good to Michael, gave him a start in the business. So, I guess I'm biased. I want to try and speak to Anton." Cassie looked toward a police car idling in the parking lot. "I'll see if I can catch a ride to the station."

"Wait a minute, are you sure that you want to talk to Anton?" Tessa caught her arm. "I've known him a lot longer."

"I know, but that may be exactly the problem. At least when I speak to him, I will be looking at him with a fresh pair of eyes, and no history between us. What do you think?" Cassie met Tessa's eyes. "It's worth a try right?"

"You may be right. You can see if you can get an update from Ollie, too." Tessa frowned. "He hasn't been replying to my texts."

"I'll let you know whatever I find out." Cassie

patted Harry and the goats, who were all inside the pen. She waved down the police officer in the parking lot that had just opened his car door. "Patrick. Are you going to the station?"

"I am."

"Can I get a ride there, please?"

"Sure Cassie." Patrick got inside and popped open the passenger side door for her. "I think someone's looking for you, though." He pointed out a man that walked through the crowd toward them.

"Cassie!" Sebastian waved to her and quickened his pace.

"No time right now." Cassie settled in the passenger seat and patted the dashboard. "Let's go." She did her best not to look in Sebastian's direction. As her heart raced, she heard the engine start up. Only when Patrick pulled out of the parking space did she dare to look out the window.

Sebastian stood at the edge of the parking lot. His eyes met hers as Patrick drove past.

Cassie quickly looked away. Was that hurt? Frustration? Annoyance? She tried to get the look on his face out of her mind, but she couldn't.

When Cassie stepped into the police station, she sought out Oliver right away. She found him in his office, bent over an open file.

"Cassie? What are you doing here?" Oliver met her eyes.

"I wanted to see if I could speak to Anton, please." Cassie straightened her shoulders. "Just for a few minutes."

"No." Oliver's eyes narrowed as he studied her. "What would make you think I would allow something like that?"

"He's allowed visitors, isn't he?" Cassie frowned. "I just wanted to speak to him."

"Cassie, Anton's been released already, a few hours ago." Oliver sighed as he gestured for her to come farther into the room. "As I said, I was going to release him. I didn't have enough evidence to keep him. But even if he was here, I couldn't let you speak to him."

"Okay." Cassie stepped closer to his desk. "Craig is really broken up over all of this." She filled him in on the story that Craig had told her about seeing Anton and Sandy together. "I do think, if Lionel knew he was on the chopping block, that might make him a suspect, too. He's had such a low profile this whole time, I'd almost forgotten about him."

"He seems like a pretty calm guy, but his career is built from this one show." Oliver nodded. "I'll speak to Craig, and then I'm going to see what Lionel has to say. Thanks for the information, Cassie."

"I just want to help." Cassie met his eyes.

"Be careful, Cassie. This isn't a game, when you get to the truth you find a killer and that killer doesn't want to be caught." Oliver snapped the file shut.

"I will be." Cassie watched as he picked up his jacket. He delivered every movement with determination. As curious as she was about who killed Sandy, she knew that his motivation ran much deeper.

Cassie wanted to solve the murder, to give Christmas back to Little Leaf Creek, to give Sandy some closure, to give herself some peace of mind, but Oliver had to solve the murder. It was his job and he certainly was dedicated to it.

CHAPTER 24

"Hey there." Tessa leaned her head through her car window and smiled at Cassie. "I thought you might need a ride."

"Seriously?" Cassie grinned as she pulled open the passenger door. "How do you always know?" Harry leaned his head through the front seats and licked Cassie's cheek. She patted his head and rubbed behind his ears.

"I heard that Anton had already been released and I figured that you wouldn't be with Ollie for too long." Tessa looked over at her. "I wanted to be here when you came out. We need to clear something up between us."

"Oh?" Cassie buckled her seat belt and let out a slow breath.

"You're right."

"What?" Cassie's eyes widened. "When am I ever right?"

"Very funny." Tessa grinned, then tightened her grip on the steering wheel. "It pains me to say this, but I shouldn't have gotten involved with anything between you and Sebastian. That's your business, and I need to leave the two of you to it."

"Thanks Tessa." Cassie relaxed against her seat.

"Did you get anything from Ollie?" Tessa backed the jeep out of the parking spot and headed toward the road.

Cassie explained what Oliver had told her.

"Do you think Anton is innocent?" Cassie looked over at Tessa.

"I think he had every opportunity to kill Sandy, as he often worked closely with her. I'm not sure why he would choose to do it on his parents' property, in his hometown." Tessa shook her head. "It doesn't seem like a smart move to me."

"Maybe not, but he would have known that he could hide the rug in the compost pile." Cassie bit into her bottom lip as she considered the possibilities. "Honestly, I don't think that any of the other suspects would know about that. As far as we know, no one else is particularly close with Anton. So, how would they know about the compost pile?"

"It didn't take long to find the compost." Tessa glanced over at her. "What do you think? Do you think he did it?"

"I think it's possible." Cassie frowned. "But if he's been released I doubt there's enough evidence."

"Hopefully, something will surface." Tessa turned onto the road. "I have some important information for you, too."

"You do?"

"Yes, I spoke to one of my contacts at the medical examiner's office and it looks like Sandy was hit over the head before she was strangled, it looks like she passed out before she was strangled." Tessa looked through the windshield. "She was knocked out."

"Knocked out." Cassie nodded. "Wow, that changes things."

"Yes, if she was knocked out she would have been killed easily." Tessa turned onto a side road. "Which of course makes narrowing down the suspects more difficult, because it makes it clear that even a small or weak person could have carried out the attack without much resistance from Sandy even though apparently she was trained in martial arts."

"That's frustrating." Cassie sighed. "That puts Heather and Nel back squarely in the suspect pool."

"Anyone could really be a suspect."

"It feels like we're back at square one."

"Maybe that's where we need to start then." Tessa drove through town in the direction of Kelvin's house. "I think we should speak to Kelvin again. Kelvin could have easily pulled off the murder himself. He lives around here. Maybe he's been in Anton's house before. Also, he is likely the source of those hateful comments. I don't think Heather would have left them, if she hoped to get Sandy to accept her pitch for a show. Sandy only upset her after some of those comments were made. Kelvin's had the longest time to fester over what she did to him, and to plan his revenge. He also had plenty to gain from the source of the lawsuits filed against him, being eliminated."

"All of that is true, but Craig still had his heart broken. Nel could have killed her to get rid of her, and also to get a promotion." Cassie shrugged. "And we can't entirely rule out Heather either."

"Maybe not, but Craig and Nel were never in Anton's house, as far as we know. Heather might have been, though, since she's a local like Kelvin. There's still the possibility that the two of them worked together somehow. Let's just talk to him one more time and see if anything comes of it." Tessa parked the jeep in front of Kelvin's house. The house was rundown, the facade cracked and the garden neglected.

Kelvin was sitting in a chair at a small table on his front porch.

"Alright, but there's no guarantee he will talk to us." Cassie stepped out of the jeep.

"Oh, I think he's warming up to me." Tessa winked. She and Harry followed Cassie up the steps.

"Oh no, you two." Kelvin groaned the moment he saw them. "I think you both need to get lives, and leave me alone."

"Come on, Kelvin, I know you're not telling the whole truth." Tessa rubbed Harry's head as he sat down next to her. Both Tessa and Harry looked at Kelvin.

Cassie blinked, then looked at Tessa. She had no idea what she thought Kelvin was lying about.

"You know nothing." Kelvin looked between Cassie and Tessa. "I'm not lying, I didn't kill her."

"I didn't say you did." Tessa smiled slightly as she walked closer to the table he sat at. "It's time you told the truth, Kelvin. You've been holding that secret in for too long."

"I don't have any secrets." Kelvin huffed as he pushed his half-empty cup of coffee across the table.

"Just tell me." Tessa smiled. "You can fight this as much as you want, but the truth will come out, it's better if you're honest about it."

"What does it matter?" Kelvin shrugged. "She was a terrible woman. She got what she deserved." He sank back down in his chair. "Why should another life be ruined just because she's gone?"

"You know who did this?" Tessa raised her voice slightly.

"And I am not telling you." Kelvin stared at her. "What do you plan to do with your bum leg and your senior discount card?"

"If you know who did this, you should say." Cassie stepped up beside Tessa. "Surely, you want a murderer caught. Even if you don't miss Sandy, you don't really think she should have been killed. Do you?"

"Oh, forgive me if I'm not intimidated by you." Kelvin chuckled, then wiped his hand across his face. "Look, if you want to tell Oliver, then tell him. I won't ever admit to it. So what if I wasn't at home like I said I was? So what if I was at a bar? It makes no difference, does it?"

Cassie noticed the faint twitch in his lips. "What

aren't you telling us, Kelvin? This is your chance to clear your name, why hesitate?"

"Because I don't need to clear it. There's no evidence against me. Oliver can threaten me all he wants, but he has nothing on me, and he knows it. So, why should I tell him anything else?" Kelvin rolled his eyes. "It's not like the police have ever done me any favors."

"Maybe you should tell him, or us, so that a killer is caught?" Tessa looked into his eyes. "Do you really want some murderer roaming free in Little Leaf Creek?"

"Look, as far as I'm concerned, the killer did me a favor." Kelvin shrugged. "With Sandy out of the way, maybe I can finally start living the life that was taken from me. The life she took from me."

"But what if the murderer kills someone else?" Cassie asked. "Surely you don't want that."

"This is pointless." Tessa sighed as she glanced over at Cassie. "I'm sure the police will get to the truth once they know he lied to them."

"Alright, alright!" Kelvin held up his hands. "It's not like I have anything to hide. I was at Fred's bar that night because I was so angry with Sandy. Her being here brought the past, what she did to me, back to the surface, that much is true. But I didn't want to kill her. Are you kidding me? With my luck? There was no way I wouldn't get caught. I did want to ruin her though, and get her off of my back once and for all. So, I decided to follow the biggest star that came with her to Little Leaf Creek, and dig up some dirt on him, or on Sandy. Anything that could ruin her life or her career. I spotted Lionel headed for Fred's bar, so I went in after him. Like I said, I just wanted to find out some information, and boy did I."

"So, tell us." Tessa looked into his eyes. "What did you find out?"

"I am telling you." Kelvin scowled at her as he sat back in his chair. "He seemed upset, he was downing drinks like crazy. So, I sat down at the table with him. After a few minutes I brought up Sandy. He went into a rage, said she was the worst producer he ever worked with, and she was out to get him. I shared my story with him, we started comparing notes. Then the door banged open, and I mean banged open, and this guy barrels in. He demands that Lionel go with him. Lionel resisted a bit, but then agreed. I wasn't about to get in the middle of anything with those two."

"Who was the other guy?" Cassie frowned. "Did Lionel say his name?"

"Yes, it was Simon I think." Kelvin shrugged. "The two took off and that was that."

"Simon?" Cassie's heart pounded. "He was at the bar with Lionel?"

"For a minute, before they both took off." Kelvin shrugged.

"Around what time were they there?" Tessa stared into his eyes.

"Wait a minute." Kelvin scowled at her. "You didn't know any of this, did you? You came here like you knew everything, but you didn't, did you?"

"It doesn't matter, now. Now, I know everything. So, tell me when you saw them leave." Tessa kept her gaze locked on him.

"Tricky, very tricky." Kelvin sighed. "It was around one or a bit after, I guess. The bar was open a bit later than it should have been." He lowered his voice. "Another reason I didn't tell Oliver. I didn't want to get anyone in trouble."

"But Lionel might have killed Sandy!" Cassie gasped. "How could you not say anything? How could you let a murderer go free?"

"Have you heard anything I just said?" Kelvin shook his head. "She got what she deserved. If you stick your little cop friend on me, I'll tell him I never said a word of any of this, so don't bother trying to use me as a witness." He finished his drink and turned to walk into his house.

Tessa steered Cassie back off the porch.

"Forget it, Cassie. He's not going to see things from your point of view. Now, we need to get to Lionel before he skips town."

"What about the goats?" Cassie frowned.

"I already took them home. It was getting too cold for all of the animals, so they closed the petting zoo early. It looks like this snow forecast might not be so crazy after all." Tessa got into the jeep. "Are you up for hunting down Lionel?"

"Absolutely. He comes off as so calm, but he wasn't calm when Kelvin was with him. At least according to Kelvin, he wasn't. His brother came to get him during the window of time that Sandy was murdered. That might mean something." Cassie settled in the passenger seat. "I just hope the RV is still where we saw it last."

"I hope so."

CHAPTER 25

essa drove toward the campground.

As Cassie watched the scenery pass by, a sigh escaped her lips.

"What is it?" Tessa glanced at her.

"Kelvin could still be guilty, couldn't he? If he left after Lionel and Simon did, he could have gotten to Sandy in time to kill her. What if he's just throwing Lionel under the bus to save himself?" Cassie pointed through the windshield. "There, the RV is still there."

"It doesn't look like anyone is home, though." Tessa parked quite close to the RV. "All of the windows are dark."

"I wonder how they get around? I didn't notice a

car here last time." Cassie peered through the window at the RV.

A rumble of engines drew their attention to the entrance of the campground. Two motorcycles roared up to the RV and stopped.

"I guess we just found out." Tessa popped her door open.

Cassie stepped out of the jeep as the two men pulled off their helmets.

"Ah, my biggest fans." Lionel grinned. "Do you want an autograph or something?"

"Actually, yes." Cassie flashed him a smile. "For my friend, Mirabel." She had been wanting to ask him for one but hadn't found the right opportunity.

"From the diner? For her?" Lionel met her eyes. "Anything." He pulled a piece of paper out of his pocket and scribbled his signature across the back of it. "I added my number. Tell her, if she wants more than an autograph, to call me."

"Real smooth, Lionel." Simon rolled his eyes. "Hooking up with some random waitress in a nothing little town is going to do wonders for your career."

"She runs the place. Remember?" Lionel swatted at him, then shook his head. "Sorry about my brother, he has no class."

"Actually, we came here to talk to you, Lionel." Tessa focused on him. Out of the corner of her eye she noticed Simon give Harry a pat, then head for the RV.

"Sure. But let's go inside, it's so chilly out here." Lionel tipped his head toward the RV. "You can bring in the dog."

Cassie hesitated. If Lionel hadn't thought twice about murdering Sandy, was it really safe to go inside with him? She felt much safer knowing Harry was with them.

"Great." Tessa looked back at Cassie and gave her a slight nod. "We can't stay long. Cassie's boyfriend is planning to meet her for dinner."

Cassie knew that Tessa was only using the ruse to make it seem like people would miss them if they didn't come back out of the RV, but a part of her wished it was true. She missed Sebastian.

"Nice." Lionel opened up the door for them. As he did, Simon bolted out past him.

"I'm going to run into town. My wallet must have fallen out of my pocket."

"Maybe, if you hadn't lost the tether I got you, you wouldn't have lost your wallet." Lionel laughed. "My kid brother would forget his head if it wasn't attached."

"Kid brother?" Cassie stepped into the RV behind him. "You two don't look too far apart in age."

"We aren't. He's only two years younger than me. But I like to make him remember he's still the younger one." Lionel gestured to a small sitting area near the front of the RV. "I know it's not much, but hopefully you can make yourselves comfortable."

"That's quite accommodating of you." Tessa settled into one of the chairs.

"I never expected it to get this cold. Once the police let us leave, Simon and I have talked about heading south while all this gets sorted out, so that we can soak up some sun." Lionel sat across from Tessa as Cassie took one of the other chairs. "So, what is it that you want to talk to me about?"

"We heard there were some issues between you and Sandy." Tessa sat back in her chair as she gazed at Lionel. Harry lay down at her feet.

"Really." Lionel settled into his own chair, his body relaxed and his tone calm. "I didn't have any issues with Sandy. If she had some issues with me, she hadn't told me about them. Not directly, anyway."

"So, you heard that she had issues with you?" Tessa held his gaze. "You were aware that she intended to get you off the show?"

"I knew about it, yes." Lionel looked between the two of them, then settled on Tessa. "I knew that she was tired of me. She didn't like the fact that I kept to myself, that I didn't engage in the kind of lifestyle the rest of the actors did. She would always invite me to parties, or out for drinks and when I refused, she acted like it was some kind of personal insult." He rolled his eyes. "I warned Craig, when he claimed that she had turned over a new leaf, that she was never going to follow through with it. But that lovesick puppy really believed her."

"Didn't that make you angry?" Cassie noticed his eyes narrow. "To think that you worked so hard, that you took your job so seriously, and in the end she was going to fire you for it?"

"Angry?" Lionel shook his head as a soft laugh escaped his lips. "I wasn't angry. I knew when I started this role that it wouldn't last forever. Whenever you need to freshen up a show, someone has to get killed off, who better than the main character's best friend? His partner? I was prepared for this day to come."

"So, you never tried to talk her out of it?" Tessa frowned. "Not even once? You didn't decide to go to her and suggest that she change her mind? You didn't plead with her to give you another chance?"

"No way." Lionel's jaw clenched. "I would never cheapen myself that way. Maybe, she didn't want me in the show anymore. That didn't mean I would lose everything. I could easily find another role to play. So no, I would never grovel for her approval. In fact, that's probably why she didn't want me around. I was the only one who wasn't scared of her."

"Maybe you weren't scared of her. Maybe you were scared of losing your job." Cassie shrugged.

"Look, I had nothing to do with her murder." Lionel looked into her eyes. "You can believe what you want, but I am a good person. I am a good person, I live a good life, I would never harm Sandy or anyone else for that matter."

"You left the bar, with your brother during the window of time that Sandy was killed, and you were upset." Tessa leaned forward slightly.

"Yes, but that means nothing." Lionel shrugged. "Yes, I was in that bar. But I never went to see Sandy. I left with Simon because I don't usually drink, and he warned me that a fan might see me, that I would end up in the papers the next morning. So, I listened to him, and I came back here."

"But why were you upset? Why were you drinking in the first place if you were perfectly okay with being written out of the show?" Cassie raised an eyebrow.

"Okay, so maybe I wasn't perfectly okay with it." Lionel shrugged. "But honestly, I wasn't upset about that. I was upset with the way that Sandy was treating Anton and his parents. Family is everything to me, and I had to watch Anton tell his parents that they probably weren't going to get any money for the shoot, since it was going to cost Sandy so much to get the place in shape. They love that house so much, and according to Anton, they are going to lose it. I offered to give him some money, but he refused. He walked me through the place, telling me about the memories he had there. I asked him why he didn't just take care of things himself, he said he was in debt himself, and hadn't been able to get out of it." He sighed, then sat back in his chair again. "It's just exhausting to think about how hard life is for some people."

"It can be." Cassie nodded, relieved that he seemed to have relaxed a bit.

"It was a rough night all around. I'd spent some time with Craig, too. In fact, right before I went to the bar, I had talked Craig out of drinking away his pain. He's been sober so long, I didn't want him to throw it all away over Sandy." Lionel looked up at

Tessa. "You can believe what you want. I know I didn't do this, and I know there are no shortage of suspects. Sorry, but I have something to do now."

"Okay. Thanks for your time."

They stepped out of the RV.

"Do you believe him?" Cassie joined Tessa and Harry in the jeep. She shivered as Tessa started the engine.

"I believe he lied before, and he could easily be lying again. Let's get back to the house and get some warmer clothes. I have a feeling this is going to turn into a long night." Tessa frowned.

"I think you're right." Cassie rubbed the thin sleeves that covered her arms.

"I can also drop Harry at home and feed him." Tessa laughed as Harry barked. "I know, you must be hungry."

When Tessa parked in her driveway, Cassie stepped out of the jeep and headed for her own house. She slid her key into the lock, and heard a soft creak. Her heart jumped into her throat as she recognized it as the sound of the rocking chair a few feet away from her.

"Cassie, don't be scared!" A deep voice spoke up from the rocking chair.

"Craig?" Cassie peered through the darkness at him.

"I'm sorry for just turning up here, but I need to speak to you again." Craig stood up from the rocking chair. "Can we go inside, it's freezing out here?"

Cassie glanced toward Tessa's house, just in time to see her door close. If Craig had something to confess to her, she didn't want to do anything to distract him.

"Of course, come inside." Cassie pushed the door open, and let him step in first. "How did you know where I live?"

"I asked some locals." Craig shrugged. "Everyone's so friendly around here."

"What do you want to tell me, Craig?" Cassie pushed the door shut, but lingered near it, with her phone in one hand. She had known Craig from when he was a child, but she didn't really know him now. She had no idea if he was capable of murder.

"Did you speak to the police about what I told you, yet?"

"No, I haven't had the chance. I hoped that you would."

"I haven't yet, because I didn't tell you the truth. I'm sorry. I can't keep it to myself anymore. I think I need to tell the truth. I know if I don't I am going to get into more trouble."

"What really happened?"

"When I saw Sandy with Anton, I was so angry." Craig wiped his palms across his face. "I hate to think that the last time we were together, she saw me so furious. I grabbed the glasses and I threw them on the floor. She had promised me that she was going to stop drinking and stay sober with me. But then she just turned around and betrayed me, like it was nothing. How was I supposed to react to that?"

"So, it wasn't Anton that broke the glasses?" Cassie's eyes widened.

"No, it wasn't him. It was me. Sandy wasn't happy about it. She told me to get out." Craig sighed. "I tried to clean up some of the glass, but I cut my hand. She wouldn't even let me wash it off. She made me leave, threatened to call the police if I didn't."

"And you washed your hand off with the hose outside?" Cassie frowned. "I guess that explains the blood on the faucet."

"Look, I know that everyone is pointing fingers at me. I can't blame them really. It'll be quite a scandal to see me on trial for Sandy's murder. But I didn't do this. Every time I say that, I seem to get buried deeper. So, I think the best thing is to tell the truth." Craig shook his head.

"Yes, if you tell the truth you can be eliminated as a suspect." Cassie looked into his eyes. "And it's the best chance of getting the real murderer caught. Don't you want that?"

"I do. Of course I do." Craig leaned forward. "But what can I do? I don't know who killed her. I have no idea what happened."

"Didn't you see anything else while you were out

there? Something that might indicate who did this?" Cassie studied him for a long moment.

"I couldn't tell the police of course, because they didn't know I was out there. But when I was leaving, I saw a motorcycle coming down the road and turn onto Anton's property." Craig narrowed his eyes. "I should have done something to help her. Like I said, I might as well be the one who gets locked up."

"Do you know whose motorcycle it was? What it looked like?" Cassie took a step toward him.

"No, I don't. It was so dark." Craig shook his head. "I just heard it, saw the lights from a distance."

"Craig, you need to speak to the police. You need to tell them everything. It's the only way they will find her murderer." Cassie met his eyes. "Do you want me to take you to the station?"

"No, that's okay. I'll go down there now." Craig nodded. "I have my car parked down the street. You're right, I'll go talk to them. Thanks Cassie."

Cassie opened the door and watched him walk toward the street. She would have to follow up with Oliver to make sure he had spoken to him.

Cassie grabbed her coat, and ran through the gate that led to Tessa's house. She had just mounted the bottom step, when Tessa pushed open the door.

"Tessa, you're not going to believe who was on

my front porch!" Cassie rushed to tell her what Craig had confessed.

"He heard a motorcycle?" Tessa narrowed her eyes. "We know two men who ride motorcycles."

"Yes, we do. Lionel and Simon. It doesn't necessarily make either of them the killers, but it's a lead."

"We should go to Anton's place and look for any motorcycle tracks that might have been left behind."

"Won't Oliver look for that once he's spoken to Craig?" Cassie looked over at her.

"He will, I'm sure, but he will have to take his statement and everything first." Tessa shrugged. "There's no harm in us going there as well, is there?"

"I guess not, no."

Tessa looked up at the brooding sky.

"It looks like terrible weather is on its way, but if we have enough time, we might be able to find some proof that Lionel and Simon were the ones who did this."

"What proof?" Cassie shook her head. "It feels like we're running around in circles. I've been sure that it was Craig, then Heather and Kelvin, and now Lionel and Simon? How can we be sure?"

"We can't be, that's why we have to go out there." Tessa grabbed her arm and steered her toward the jeep. "There is no such thing as the perfect murder. A murderer always leaves a clue behind. The problem is, we haven't been looking in the right place for it."

"Maybe not, but we're not the only ones that have been looking, Ollie hasn't found anything either." Cassie settled in the passenger side.

"He just needs a little help from his friends." Tessa started the jeep.

As Tessa drove back toward the house, Cassie's phone buzzed.

She read a text from Sebastian.

Hi Cassie. Would love to catch up tomorrow.

A small smile reached Cassie's lips. Maybe he had found someone new to be in a relationship with, but there might still be hope for their friendship to survive the whole mess. She looked up as Tessa turned down the road that led to the property.

"If it was Lionel, maybe that's why he was drinking in the bar that night, he knew what he was about to do, or wanted an alibi. He's certainly strong enough to get the body to the shed." Cassie shook her head. "I can't believe I didn't see this from the beginning. He's always so open, he played it so cool. Of course he was trying to hide something."

"He didn't want to be fired. It's as simple as that.

He knew if he got rid of Sandy, Nel would keep him on." Tessa turned down the driveway and drove toward the house.

"I saw how comfortable they were together at the diner, before any of this happened. He and Nel are friends. I'm sure she would have kept him on the show." As soon as the jeep stopped, Cassie stepped out. She turned on the flashlight on her phone, and swept the exterior of the house. Her heart skipped a beat as her light played over a motorcycle parked in the driveway.

"Tessa, we're not alone out here."

"Who do you think it is?" Tessa stepped around the front of the jeep and stood beside Cassie.

"It could be Lionel, or even his brother, Simon, right?" Cassie frowned.

"Why would either of them be out here, though?"

"I'm not sure, but we shouldn't stick around to find out." Cassie grabbed her arm. "We need to get back in the jeep and call Ollie. He should be the one handling this."

"Really Cassie?" Tessa shook her arm free. "This is our chance. We might be able to find real evidence of what the killer is up to. Maybe he came back to try to cover his tracks, and we can catch him in the act."

"I don't know, Tessa, it's risky, isn't it." Cassie looked over the motorcycle as she shook her head. "You should at least let Ollie know what's going on."

"Let's just have a look around." Tessa turned toward Cassie. "We can call him afterwards. We don't want to bother him for nothing."

"Okay, let's see if we can find out where the owner of this motorcycle is. We don't want to draw any attention to ourselves." Cassie peered up at the house. "I don't see any lights on inside. Maybe the killer is out here somewhere."

"Or he turned the lights out when he heard the jeep coming." Tessa walked around the side of the house. "There's no time to waste. We might be able to surprise him if we go in through the back. You take the other side, and we'll meet up in the back."

Cassie's heart raced as she walked around the side of the house. She still wasn't convinced that Lionel had killed Sandy, but she sensed that whoever did wasn't far away. She neared the back of the house, with her muscles tense and her flashlight pointed at the ground. Although the ground was still dry, she noticed a few scuff marks in the dirt near the corner of the house. She guessed that whoever made them had done so not long before. She turned off her flashlight and crouched down close to the corner. As her eyes adjusted to the darkness, she noticed a figure not far from the back porch. A person, whose face was covered by a motorcycle helmet.

Cassie froze as the person grabbed the helmet and began to tug it off.

Was she about to see the face of Sandy's killer?

As the helmet pulled free, long blonde hair poured down around the woman's shoulders.

Cassie took a sharp breath. Of all the people she had expected to be hidden behind the helmet, she was not one of them.

"Stephanie?" Cassie took a step back as the woman turned toward her.

"Who's there?" Stephanie pointed a flashlight toward Cassie. "How do you know my name? Were you following me?"

"No, I wasn't following you. What are you doing out here?" Cassie glanced around for any sign of Sebastian. "Are you meeting someone out here?"

"That's not really any of your business, is it?" Stephanie glared at Cassie. "What are you doing here?"

"Looking for a murderer." Tessa stepped up behind Stephanie. "You wouldn't know anything about that, would you?"

"Are you talking about Sandy?" Stephanie frowned. "Of course, I don't know anything about who killed Sandy. Why would I?"

"Do you always ride a motorcycle?" Cassie's heart raced. She couldn't shake the memory of Sebastian telling Stephanie that he loved her. What was it about her that Sebastian liked so much? Clearly, she was a few years younger. Maybe, it was the fact that she had a motorcycle. Maybe, Cassie was just too boring for him. But had Sebastian fallen for a murderer?

"Yes, I always do." Stephanie rested the helmet on her hip, then stared at her. "What are you two supposed to be? Some kind of amateur detectives? Or are you trying out for a part on the show?"

"Does Sebastian know you're here?" Cassie raised an eyebrow.

"He doesn't need to know." Stephanie rolled her eyes. "You need to get out of here." She looked toward a path that led away from the house through the woods, out toward the road. "I'm waiting for someone."

"Who?" Tessa looked down the path as well. "Who are you here to meet?"

"Like I said, it's none of your business." Stephanie

flipped her hair over her shoulder, then walked toward the path.

"Wait, Stephanie!" Cassie felt a sudden urgency to protect her, even after seeing her with Sebastian. If he did love her, as he said he did, then she needed to make sure that Stephanie got back to him in one piece. "Whoever it is that you're meeting, you should cancel it. We're close to figuring out who killed Sandy, this is a dangerous place for you to be."

"What?" Stephanie turned back to face Cassie. "If you know who killed her, then why not go to the police? Why are you out here in such a dangerous place?"

"That's a very good question." A stern voice carried through the crisp air, just as a snowflake drifted down in front of Cassie's face. "Don't do anything stupid, or I'll shoot."

"It's snowing." Cassie uttered the words even as her body tensed with fear.

"Cassie, stay where you are." Tessa's voice wavered as she spoke. Cassie was shocked at the uneasiness in Tessa's voice. Tessa was nervous, which made Cassie more nervous.

Cassie heard a subtle crunch as the person behind her stepped closer.

"Everyone stay put." The man demanded. "I

might not be able to hit all of you, but I can guarantee you I will get one of you."

"Simon," Cassie whispered his name as she tried to resist turning to face him. "Simon, it was you?"

"Keep quiet!" Simon barked his words right beside her ear.

"Don't!" Cassie held up her hands. "Don't do this, you're never going to get away with it."

"Get away with it?" Simon laughed as he walked around in front of her. "I almost did. Anton was about to go away for life for Sandy's murder. Nel would have taken over as producer, and Lionel's role would have become bigger, instead of ended." He winced as he tightened his grip on the gun. "I planned this, so carefully. I took the opportunity to do what had to be done, and although I didn't think I'd ever be capable of it, I did it. I killed a woman just to stop my brother from losing his job. But Stephanie messed it all up."

"I didn't mean to. It wasn't my fault." Stephanie shivered as she edged a little closer to Cassie.

"What do you mean?" Cassie took a deep breath. More snowflakes began to fall. It would have been magical, were it not for the barrel of the gun they landed on.

"I mean, I wanted to be part of the show. Really

bad." Stephanie's voice wavered. "I'm an actress, or at least I want to be one, and this was my last chance to get a break. I'm thirty-five now, and it's hard to even get an audition. I thought maybe if I showed up in Little Leaf Creek, I could get Sandy to just give me an audition. I thought I'd check out the property where the episode was going to be filmed. It was after midnight. I never thought anyone would be here at that time. But when I got here, I saw Simon coming out of the house. He was acting weird. He said Sandy wasn't here. After the murder, I went to speak to him about why he was here that night, about what he knew. I thought maybe he had seen something, I didn't really think he was the murderer, but then he threatened me. He wanted me to keep quiet about seeing him here."

Cassie realized that Simon went to get Lionel from the bar after he had killed Sandy.

"I think I know why you did this." Cassie shot a glare at Simon as he walked around her. "Why you murdered Sandy."

"What do you know?" Simon pointed the gun directly at her. "You have no idea what I did or why!"

"I know that if Lionel lost his job you would lose out as well. You wouldn't have your precious brother to live off of?" Cassie took a sharp breath as he shifted closer to her. "You didn't have to kill her."

"You don't know anything!" Simon nearly shrieked his words. "I did everything for Lionel. I helped build his career, I supported him. If Sandy wrote him out of the show I was going to land up with nothing. All of my hard work, my years of dedication. For nothing. I just wanted her to listen to reason. But she wouldn't, I had to do something. For the good of the show, the good of the actors, the good of everyone involved."

"You didn't have to kill her." Cassie shivered as the barrel of the gun hovered inches from her face.

"Then, he would have been fired. I knew that there was only one way to keep Lionel in the show. When I told her what a mistake she was making by killing Lionel off, all she could say was that she wanted a change, that Lionel was boring, and the show needed to be livened up. She even suggested putting Craig in the role of partner. Are you kidding me? He's the worst actor on the show!" Simon waved the gun through the air as a groan escaped his lips. "She was going to ruin the entire show."

"Did Lionel help you?" Cassie asked. "Did you do this together?"

"No." Simon scowled, rage creasing his features

as he waved the gun around. "He had nothing to do with this. You leave him alone." He aimed the gun at Cassie.

"Calm down, take a breath." Tessa inched forward in an attempt to shield Cassie.

"Don't you move!" Simon swung the gun toward Tessa.

"No!" Cassie gasped. "Stop it! Don't you dare point that gun at her!"

"What are you going to do about it?" Simon pointed the gun at Cassie again. "Are you going to stop me? I'm done living in the shadows, waiting for the powerful people to make decisions about my life."

"Leave them alone!" Stephanie's voice wavered. "They're not who you came here for."

"No, they're not." Simon swung the gun toward Stephanie. "I came here for you, Stephanie, I know you knew I killed her. I know you were going to try and trip me up."

"I knew you did something when I saw you here and then I found out that Sandy had been murdered. I just didn't want to believe it." Stephanie shivered and wrapped her arms tighter around herself. "I can't believe you murdered her, just so you would keep the lifestyle you're accustomed to."

"Believe it." Simon pointed the gun straight at Stephanie. "Like I said, I'm done with other people running my life. So, if that means I have to take all three of you out, then that is exactly what I will do."

Floodlights suddenly ignited, followed by the roar of a familiar engine.

Cassie took the moment while Simon was distracted to step between him and Stephanie. In the same moment, Tessa lunged forward and attempted to wrench the gun from Simon's hands.

"Drop it!"

The engine roared again, and this time the truck rumbled forward as well. An instant later, Simon hit the ground, pinned down by Oliver while a swarm of officers surrounded him with guns drawn.

"Stay down!" Oliver's voice was almost drowned out by the sound of Sebastian's truck. But Cassie still heard it.

Tears of relief filled her eyes as Tessa stepped away from the two on the ground.

"Are you okay, Tessa?" Cassie reached for her hand.

"I'm okay." Tessa squeezed her hand. "I've still got some zip left in me, you know?"

"Cassie!" Sebastian ran through the floodlights on his truck, straight toward her.

"It's okay, Sebastian." Cassie forced herself to smile as he neared her. "Stephanie's okay, she's right there. She's okay."

Sebastian glanced over at Stephanie, held her gaze for a moment, then looked back at Cassie.

"I'm so relieved you're okay." Sebastian pulled her into his arms and before she could think to turn away, his lips crushed against hers.

For a moment, Cassie forgot that Stephanie ever existed. For a moment, she didn't notice the snowflakes that fell against her skin, because warmth flooded through her. But the moment passed. She broke the kiss and pushed him away from her.

"What are you doing?"

"Cassie, please." Sebastian stared hard into her eyes. "I don't know what happened, but whatever it is, we can work it out, I know we can."

"But." Cassie looked over at Stephanie whose focus appeared to be on Oliver and Simon. "You're in love with Stephanie."

"What?" Sebastian laughed.

"I heard you tell her that you loved her." Cassie frowned as she wondered how he could laugh at something so serious.

"Cassie." Sebastian pulled her close again, then leaned his forehead against hers. "She's my sister."

Shock rippled through Cassie as his words sunk in. All this time she'd been certain he was done with her, that he'd found someone new, and all at once she understood how mistaken she had been.

"Your sister?"

"She's always had these big dreams." Sebastian shot Stephanie a stern look. "When she heard that Inspector Heathcliffe was going to be filmed here, she insisted on coming out. But I warned her not to get involved with these people." He frowned as Oliver led Simon to a waiting police car. "It's not the lifestyle I want for her. I tried to get her to go back home." He sighed. "But she never listens to me."

"Your sister?" Cassie repeated again. Now, she could see the resemblance. She turned back to Sebastian. "I'm sorry. You must think I was acting pretty crazy."

"No, I'm sorry." Sebastian brushed her hair back from her face and looked into her eyes. "If I had dealt with it properly, there never would have been any doubt in your mind. Cassie, I'm with you. I would never betray you. Never."

As Sebastian's words rolled through her mind she felt the truth in them. He wasn't saying them, just to say them. She felt as if he meant them.

"You should get her home." Cassie looked over at Stephanie who shivered as the snow fell harder. "It's so cold out here."

"Come with me." Sebastian squeezed her hand.

"No, I think you two should have some time." Cassie looked toward the police car. "I need to talk to Ollie." She pulled her hand away, then turned back to look at him. "Sebastian, how did you know to come out here?"

"Actually, that was thanks to Stephanie." Sebastian draped an arm around his sister's shoulders. "She suspected that Simon had done something to Sandy when she saw him here. So, she came to me and eventually admitted to seeing Simon here and that he was threatening her to keep quiet. So, I decided I needed some help from a friend." He nodded to Oliver. "Oliver said that Simon claimed he was never out here. When Simon started threatening Stephanie to keep quiet about it, we helped Stephanie set the meeting up with Simon, and planned to be here to catch him threatening her and hopefully get him to confess to killing Sandy."

"Before Sebastian told me about Simon, I was sure Kelvin was the murderer. I found out that he's been leaving threatening posts against Sandy on social media for months." Oliver walked over to them. "Something tells me the two of you figured out Simon was the murderer before all of this."

"Not exactly. We had it narrowed down, at least we thought we did, but we still weren't sure." Tessa shook her head. "If Stephanie hadn't seen him here, he might never have been caught for the murder."

"I guess that he knew enough about the house, from the pictures that Anton had, and what Anton told him about it, that he was able to find the compost pile." Cassie scrunched up her nose. "Not that he couldn't have figured it out from the smell."

"Speaking of which." Stephanie looked between them. "Can we please get out of here, I don't think I can stand it a minute longer." She eyed Cassie for a moment. "I guess we'll be seeing a bit more of each other."

"Let's get you home." Sebastian frowned. "We still have a lot more to talk about."

Cassie watched the siblings walk to Sebastian's truck.

"And you two, are coming with me." Oliver pointed to his car. "We have a lot to talk about, too."

Once back at the station, Oliver herded them both into his office.

"I need to talk to Simon, but first, you need to tell me what you know." He sat on the edge of his desk.

Cassie and Tessa took turns filling him in on what they discovered.

"Oh!" Cassie gasped. "Simon lost his wallet tether, I bet that's what he used to strangle Sandy."

"I guess I will find out." Oliver pointed to the chairs in front of his desk. "Wait here, I have more that I want to say."

By the time Oliver came back, Cassie and Tessa were both prepared for his wrath.

"What you two did tonight." Oliver shook his head, then paused in front of his desk to look at them. "It was reckless, and dangerous."

"Here we go." Tessa rolled her eyes. "Don't even think about trying to lecture me, Ollie!"

"You could have jeopardized the whole investigation." Oliver crossed his arms.

"But we didn't. We helped get him talking. We helped you catch a killer." Tessa smiled. "Do you have everything you need to arrest him?"

"Yes. When I mentioned the wallet tether, he

knew I had him. He confessed to everything. He claims that his brother wasn't involved at all, and I believe him. Now go home, get some rest. Tomorrow is Christmas Eve, and I'm going to want some of those gingerbread cookies."

"I'll make sure you get some." Tessa smiled. "You make sure you get some rest."

CHAPTER 29

The next evening, Cassie helped Tessa set out platters of gingerbread cookies at the diner.

"Oh, I've got another tray in the car! I'll be right back!" Tessa hurried out the door.

Cassie smiled to herself as she noticed Tessa's excitement. It seemed to her that Tessa was getting used to being part of the community again.

"I think having a Christmas Eve celebration here was a great idea." Mirabel leaned against the counter and looked out at the sea of faces gathered at the various tables in the diner. "It's a great way to bring our community back together."

"It was an excellent idea, Mirabel." Cassie smiled

at her as she held out a small package. "I have something for you."

"What? A gift?" Mirabel grinned. "Cassie, you didn't have to do that."

"It's just a little something." Cassie shrugged. "Nothing too great, really."

"Can I open it?" Mirabel cast a guilty look in the direction of the other people. "I certainly don't have gifts to hand out."

"Don't worry about it, having the diner open is gift enough." Cassie laughed. "Now, just unwrap it already!"

Mirabel grinned and began to unwrap the gift. "Oh." She blinked, then stared at the crumpled paper. "Thanks Cassie, this is really sweet." She looked up from the receipt. "Is it some kind of memento?"

"Look on the back." Cassie laughed.

Mirabel flipped the paper over, then gasped. "Is this what I think it is? Is this Lionel's autograph?"

"Yes, it is. Not just that, but his phone number, too." Cassie grinned. "He was pretty interested in hearing from you."

"Oh Cassie!" Mirabel let out a squeal, then pulled Cassie into a tight hug. "You have just made my year, and next year, too! I can't believe I don't have anything for you!"

"There is one thing I'd like." Cassie looked into Mirabel's eyes, which still sparkled with excitement. "If you're willing to give it."

"Of course, anything." Mirabel rested her elbow on the counter and leaned on her hand. "I don't know if anyone has ever told you this, Cassie, but you're hard to buy for."

"This is something you don't have to buy. I just want an answer." Cassie continued to hold her gaze. "An honest answer."

"Alright, shoot." Mirabel stared back at her. "You're so serious, it's a little freaky."

"I want to know why you took off for the woods, Mirabel, when we found Sandy's body. I want to know why you acted like me calling the cops was such a big problem." Cassie raised an eyebrow.

"Cassie." Mirabel sighed. "I was just frightened, that's all. Not all of us can handle seeing a dead body, you know?"

"I asked for an honest answer, Mirabel." Cassie looked into her eyes. "If you're not going to tell me the truth, then just tell me that you don't want to tell me."

"Cassie, listen." Mirabel leaned closer to her. "There are things about me, things about my past, that you don't know about. Sometimes, I forget that I'm not part of that anymore. I guess, between seeing Sandy's body and hearing you say something about the police, my old instincts kicked in, and I just felt safer hiding out. I wanted to be anywhere but there. Is that enough of an answer for you?"

"It's a start, Mirabel." Cassie stared into her eyes. "But I do hope that you know I'm your friend. If there's anything you want to talk about, anything you want to tell me, you always can."

"Thanks Cassie." Mirabel smiled. "I might take you up on that one of these days. But for now that's the best I can offer."

"I understand." Arms slid around Cassie's waist and tugged her back a few steps.

"There you are!" Sebastian pulled her close and whispered in her ear. "I can't wait to get you under the mistletoe."

"Stop it." Cassie laughed as she pushed him away. "I'm working!"

"It's Christmas Eve, you shouldn't be working." Sebastian kissed her cheek. "We should be sitting in front of a fire, listening to sappy Christmas songs. Of course, since my sister is staying with me for a while, I guess that might be a bit awkward."

"That reminds me." Cassie pulled a key out of her

pocket and held it out to him. "I want to give this back to you."

"No." Sebastian curled her fingers over the key and gently pushed her hand away.

"No?" Cassie's eyes widened. "Why not?"

"Cassie, I know what we just went through was a misunderstanding. But it also showed me that maybe we need to make things clearer between us. You're the only person I want to be with, but that doesn't mean you're ready for me to have a key to your house. Even if it is just to help out with the renovations. You keep that, and give it back to me when you're ready. Okay?" Sebastian smiled a wide smile that showed his dimples. "No pressure." He settled his hand on her hip and guided her closer to him. "No rush. I'm going to make sure you know you can trust me."

"Sebastian, I do." Cassie frowned as she kissed his cheek.

"No, you don't. At least not completely." Sebastian looked into her eyes. "It's going to take some time. And that's okay, I'm here to stay."

"I like the sound of that." Cassie's cheeks flushed. Despite the thin layer of snow on the ground outside, and the unusually cold temperature for Little Leaf Creek, she was filled with warmth.

Maybe it wasn't a traditional way to spend Christmas, but there was no other place she wanted to be. It seemed to her that the people of Little Leaf Creek had their secrets, and she still had a few of her own, but that didn't stop them from being a community that looked out for each other. She caught sight of the tip jar on the counter spilling over with donations, for Anton's parents. Nothing would erase the tragedy that had occurred, but she could still feel the magic of Christmas in the laughter of those around her, and the delicious scent of gingerbread cookies.

The End

TESSA'S GINGERBREAD COOKIE RECIPE

Ingredients:

Cookies:

3/4 cup butter, at room temperature

3/4 cup light brown sugar

2/3 cup molasses

1 egg, at room temperature

1 teaspoon vanilla extract

3 1/2 cups all-purpose flour

1 teaspoon baking soda

1/4 teaspoon salt

1 tablespoon ground ginger

2 teaspoons ground cinnamon

1/4 teaspoon ground nutmeg

1/4 teaspoon ground cloves

Royal Icing:

4 cups confectioners' sugar
3 tablespoons meringue powder
4 to 8 tablespoons water
Gel food coloring, optional

Preparation:

For the cookies:

Beat the butter in an electric mixer for 2 minutes. Add the brown sugar and molasses and beat together until light and fluffy.

Beat in the lightly beaten egg and vanilla extract.

Whisk together the flour, baking soda, salt, ginger, cinnamon, nutmeg and cloves.

Gradually add the dry ingredients to the wet ingredients and mix until just combined. Don't overmix.

Form the dough into a ball. Divide into two and flatten into disks. Wrap in plastic wrap and refrigerate for at least 2 hours or overnight.

When you are ready to bake the cookies, preheat the oven to 350 degrees Fahrenheit. Line two baking sheets with parchment paper.

Roll the dough on a lightly floured surface with a lightly floured rolling pin until about 1/4-inch thick.

Using Christmas-themed cookie cutters cut out the cookies and place on the trays. Re-roll the leftover dough. If the dough gets too warm and sticky, return to the refrigerator to cool.

Bake for about 8 to 10 minutes until set, slightly browned and slightly risen. The baking time will vary depending on the size of the cookies.

Cool on the cookie trays for about 5 minutes, then transfer to a wire rack to cool completely.

For the royal icing:

Beat together the confectioners' sugar, meringue

powder and 4 tablespoons of water until stiff peaks form. Add more water if it is too thick.

If desired, add in food coloring and mix until combined.

Decorate the cookies with royal icing and leave aside to set.

Enjoy!!

ABOUT THE AUTHOR

Cindy Bell is a USA Today and Wall Street Journal Bestselling Author. She is the author of the Little Leaf Creek, Wagging Tail, Donut Truck, Dune House, Sage Gardens, Chocolate Centered, Macaron Patisserie, Nuts about Nuts, Bekki the Beautician, Heavenly Highland Inn and Wendy the Wedding Planner cozy mystery series.

Cindy has always loved reading, but it is only recently that she has discovered her passion for writing romantic cozy mysteries. She loves walking along the beach thinking of the next adventure her characters can embark on.

You can sign up for her newsletter so you are notified of her latest releases at http://www.cindybellbooks.com.

Christmas Chocolates and Crimes

Hot Chocolate and Homicide

Chocolate Caramels and Conmen

Picnics, Pies and Lies

Devils Food Cake and Drama

Cinnamon and a Corpse

Cherries, Berries and a Body

Christmas Cookies and Criminals

Grapes, Ganache & Guilt

Yule Logs & Murder

DUNE HOUSE COZY MYSTERIES

Seaside Secrets

Boats and Bad Guys

Treasured History

Hidden Hideaways

Dodgy Dealings

Suspects and Surprises

Ruffled Feathers

A Fishy Discovery

Danger in the Depths

Celebrities and Chaos

Pups, Pilots and Peril

Tides, Trails and Trouble

Racing and Robberies

Athletes and Alibis

Manuscripts and Deadly Motives

Pelicans, Pier and Poison

Sand, Sea and a Skeleton

Pianos and Prison

Relaxation, Reunions and Revenge

A Tangled Murder

WAGGING TAIL COZY MYSTERIES

Murder at Pawprint Creek (prequel)

Murder at Pooch Park

Murder at the Pet Boutique

A Merry Murder at St. Bernard Cabins

Murder at the Dog Training Academy

Murder at Corgi Country Club

A Merry Murder on Ruff Road

Murder at Poodle Place

Murder at Hound Hill

Murder at Rover Meadows

SAGE GARDENS COZY MYSTERIES

Sage Gardens Cozy Mystery Series Box Set Volume 1
(Books 1 - 4)

Birthdays Can Be Deadly

Money Can Be Deadly

Trust Can Be Deadly

Ties Can Be Deadly

Rocks Can Be Deadly

Jewelry Can Be Deadly

Numbers Can Be Deadly

Memories Can Be Deadly

Paintings Can Be Deadly

Snow Can Be Deadly

Tea Can Be Deadly

Greed Can Be Deadly

Clutter Can Be Deadly

NUTS ABOUT NUTS COZY MYSTERIES

A Tough Case to Crack

A Seed of Doubt

Roasted Peanuts and Peril

<u>Treated and Dyed</u>

<u>A Wrinkle-Free Murder</u>

A MACARON PATISSERIE COZY MYSTERY
SERIES

<u>Sifting for Suspects</u>

<u>Recipes and Revenge</u>

<u>Mansions, Macarons and Murder</u>

HEAVENLY HIGHLAND INN COZY
MYSTERIES

<u>Murdering the Roses</u>

<u>Dead in the Daisies</u>

<u>Killing the Carnations</u>

<u>Drowning the Daffodils</u>

<u>Suffocating the Sunflowers</u>

<u>Books, Bullets and Blooms</u>

<u>A Deadly Serious Gardening Contest</u>

<u>A Bridal Bouquet and a Body</u>

<u>Digging for Dirt</u>

WENDY THE WEDDING PLANNER COZY MYSTERIES

<u>Matrimony, Money and Murder</u>

<u>Chefs, Ceremonies and Crimes</u>

<u>Knives and Nuptials</u>

<u>Mice, Marriage and Murder</u>